~ Look for these titles from A. C. Fox ~

Now Available from Etopia Press

Now Available

The Warriors of Love & Magic Series

The General's Hostage (Book One)
The Captive Prince (Book Two)

Hold the Sky
"Desert Candy" Halloween Heat IV

The Captive Prince

The Warriors of Love & Magic Book Two

A. C. Fox

etopia
press

Etopia Press
1643 Warwick Ave., #124
Warwick, RI 02889
http://www.etopia-press.net

THE CAPTIVE PRINCE

Print ISBN: 978-1-944138-71-4
Digital ISBN: 978-1-944138-69-1

First Etopia Press electronic publication: November 2016

First Etopia Press print publication: November 2016

~ Dedication ~

For the librarian in Kenosha who introduced me to all those great books when I pestered her with questions of what to read next. Thank you.

CHAPTER ONE

Prince Falken stood at the narrow window in his tower room and waited to kill the man who had imprisoned him. Far below him, the rain made ripple patterns on the puddles of water all across the courtyard. Above him, the rain sounded a constant tapping on the tower roof. He'd long ago stopped truly hearing it.

It never stopped raining here. There was no sun. The clouds never parted. Day in and day out, one unending, dreary storm remained overhead, sapping all the humor and light from the world.

The rain was one of a hundred reasons why he hated this fortress. Why he loathed its moss-draped battlements and the gloom of the surrounding mountain peaks. But most of his hate he reserved for Lord Domlen Jadale. The grim-faced man was huge as a bear, with cold, dark eyes and such an aura of raw power that even a member of Teirlan royalty like Falken had to give him wary respect. Respect, but also hatred. The bastard had taken away Falken's magic, cutting him off from his power by means of two locking, spell-inscribed bracers.

Falken shifted the small but heavy decorative bust he gripped in his hands. The miniature marble sculpture was of Pherros, the god of love from Gondellan myth. It had been on a bookshelf in the lavishly appointed tower room when Lord Domlen had locked him here weeks ago. There it had sat merrily upon the bookshelf amid the leather-bound tomes of history, poetry, and legend. Mocking him. But it was heavy enough to smash a man's head in, much heavier than the split wood stacked near the fireplace, and easier to conceal from sight. Although he didn't intend for Lord Domlen to ever see him coming.

He had no other choice than to use such a crude weapon against Domlen. The bracelets locked around his wrists were made of crovmane, an ensorcelled metal that nullified magic power. A disciple of magic, he was helpless without his spells. His books of mystic lore and his laboratory were lost to him. They were hundreds of leagues away in Lindermain, the seat of the royal court in Teirlan. It was as if he'd been castrated. It made him feel helpless, weak, not a man of magic, and perhaps not a man at all...

Weakness. He hated the feeling. Physically, he'd always been the smallest of his family. His two older brothers were burly warrior-types who favored sword and lance. But Falken's magic had more than evened the odds once he'd finally come into his own. Although he abhorred being seen as frail and powerless, he hoped his captor was arrogant enough to believe a prince was nothing of a threat. A blow to the head from this stone bust would change the man's opinion in a hurry. His stomach rumbled. It was nearly time for his evening meal of slop soup. Soon Falken would have his chance at freedom.

His captor regularly brought him meals, which was strange enough as it was. Prince Falken was used to being tended by servants, but not personally fed by the lord of a stronghold. He didn't know if Domlen didn't want him in contact with the servants and guards because Falken's presence at this backwater, miserable swamp of a fortress needed to be kept secret, but it would be the man's undoing. This time, when Domlen came through the door with his food, Falken would dash his brains in. Then he would flee the tower, escape through a postern gate or the fortress's sewers. There definitely had to be sewers or moat-channels to drain off all this cursed water that fell from the sky without ceasing.

Either way, once Domlen was finished and Falken was beyond the walls, he was confident he could find his way back to his homeland. When his father, King Nikolen, learned the third son of his line had been kidnapped and held captive, he would bring the full might of Teirlan down on this obscure borderland fortress and erase it from the map. Even if his father cared little for him, the king could not allow such an insult and an act of war to go unanswered.

Unless his father had orchestrated the kidnapping in the first place. Or one of his brothers, Tobias or Yeznon, had ordered it done as part of some political scheme, perhaps a move against the sorcerers of Lindermain...

He rubbed at one of the symbol-covered metal bracers on his wrists and shook his head. He had no time now to brood over the backstabbing politics of the royal court. Movement in the rain-drenched courtyard below attracted his eye. He leaned closer to the window, angling for a good view without drawing attention.

A young man carrying a spear and wearing chain mail and leather walked under the arching battlements, careful to stay out of the rain. Falken recognized the guard because he'd seen the man on his rounds before, but he'd never spoken to him. Except for Lord Domlen, he'd never spoken to anyone in this fortress since he'd been imprisoned here. His entire world consisted of this one tower room, twenty paces by twenty paces, with a window facing east and another west. If it weren't for the surrounding mountains and the constant, low ceiling of clouds, he could've at least watched the dawn and the setting sun. But even that was denied him.

He switched his makeshift weapon to his other hand and watched as the guard ducked into a little alcove and set his spear aside. A moment later, a woman dressed in servant's garb hurried along the same path the guard had taken. She turned aside into the alcove as well. Falken couldn't help a smile as he watched the two furtively glance around the courtyard and then embrace. Potential enemies or not, there was something about them that warmed him deep inside, enough that he no longer noticed the damp, cold air creeping through the window. The guard touched her chin and gently titled her head to give him easier access to her lips. The girl was pretty, true enough, but personally, Falken would've been more interested in the guard. He'd always preferred the company of men for loveplay.

The two lovers broke apart quickly when Lord Domlen entered the courtyard and moved into Falken's view. Domlen's boots slammed down into the puddles, sending up gouts of water as he stomped through the downpour. At the sight of him, Falken's heart began to beat faster, hollow booms resounding in his chest like a man pounding on a door. The enormity of what he was about to do swept over him.

He had never killed anyone before. Not in war or in self-defense. And he wouldn't even be using the magic he'd trained and studied with; he would be using his hands. Now that the time had arrived, he realized he was terrified. He felt as if he might be sick to his stomach at any moment.

No, he had to be strong. He had to be a true prince of the Teirlan royal line. He might not relish this bloodshed, but he was desperate. After all this time trapped here without his magic, he was closer to a cornered animal than a royal prince. If there had been a ransom demand sent back to Teirlan, it had not been met. There had been no promise of release if Falken met certain terms or fulfilled certain oaths. There was only this tower. And there was only Lord Domlen, the man who kept him here.

Below him in the courtyard, Domlen spotted the two lovers in their alcove and paused to greet them, though Falken's tower room was far too high to hear his words. They bowed to him. Domlen continued across the courtyard toward the tower, pulling his dark cloak closer around him. As always, he was carrying a covered, silver serving tray with Falken's dinner.

No turning back now. He hurried to the room's heavy, iron-banded door and readied his makeshift weapon. When Domlen set foot inside, Falken would ambush him and end this once and for all.

The waiting was torture as he listened for the sound of Domlen's boots on the tower's spiraling stone staircase. Soon enough he recognized Domlen's heavy tread. He raised the bust over his head. His hands were shaking. His mouth felt dry as a desert.

Domlen's footfalls reached the door. There was a pause.

Falken could imagine Domlen shifting the covered serving dish to his other hand. Imagine him reaching for the door handle...

The handle rattled as Domlen used his key to unlock it. Falken didn't even risk a breath. He was completely focused on his attack. The heavy door swung open. Lord Domlen stepped inside.

"Prince Falken, your meal is—" Domlen began to say, but then Falken stepped out from behind the door and swung the bust at his head.

Lord Domlen reacted instantaneously. He shoved the serving tray at Falken, driving it into the path of Falken's blow. Scalding-hot soup spilled all over him. The unexpected counterattack completely threw off Falken's aim. Instead of crushing Domlen's head, his attack put a huge dent in the serving tray cover and sent it careening against the wall.

Falken hissed in pain as the hot liquid burned him, soaking through his breeches and into his tunic. Fear reached up to choke him as Domlen's cold stare found him and held him. How had he missed? The man couldn't have seen the attack coming.

The depth of his desperation threatened to drown him as he realized his best chance at escape was quickly evaporating. Or was already gone. He tried to recover and press his attack, even though he'd lost the element of surprise—his single advantage with his magic lost to him.

Domlen easily blocked the second attack. His block hit Falken's forearm so hard that the stone bust flew out of his hands and shattered against the floor. He snarled a curse and tried to punch his captor in the jaw.

Again, Domlen swept aside his blow almost contemptuously. But this time Domlen grabbed him by the front of his tunic and hurled him across the room. Falken hit the floor hard and slid along the stone surface until he crashed into the writing table.

Lord Domlen eyed him coldly. Falken lay there in a heap where he'd been thrown, panting hard, momentarily stunned. The blow to his ego had hurt far more than the pain of hitting the ground. He pushed himself to a sitting position, watching the other man warily. There would certainly be reprisals and punishment. He didn't believe Domlen would kill him for the ambush. After all, he must have some value, or why keep him alive in this tower? But he expected a severe beating or worse.

But Domlen only closed the door behind him without a word. He turned to scowl at the spilled food and the dented serving dish. Then he walked over and picked up the tray.

Under other circumstances, Prince Falken might have found his captor attractive in his way, certainly *memorable*. Domlen wore a cloak so purple it was nearly black. His doublet was black slashed with gray. His breeches matched the color, tucked into knee-high leather boots still wet from outside and gleaming in the candlelight Falken used to drive off the gloom. A single gold chain adorned his neck, with a golden sword pendant set along a symbol Falken didn't recognize. His rings were plain gold. His face, however, was the face of a hard, merciless man.

Domlen's eyes were the same dark gray as the storm clouds that plagued this land. His jaw was as rigid as a shield, his dark hair kept short, his shoulders almost twice as wide as Falken's. The man's face resembled something chiseled out of a mountainside by an artist with more enthusiasm than talent. Everything about him gave off a sense of power, strength, and ruthlessness. He had the look of a leader who had seen war and hadn't yielded.

Had Falken truly believed he could defeat this man so easily, without access to his magic? His lips twisted into a sour smile. He'd been desperate. Still was. Desperate men fooled themselves better than anyone.

It didn't matter now. His gambit had failed. His captor was frighteningly strong. He'd flung Falken across the room as if he were made of straw and easily outweighed him by at least seven stone. It would've been a different tale if Falken still had access to his magic. Domlen would be nothing more than a hated memory. But neither wishes nor ifs could help him now.

Finally, the man spoke, so emotionless the sound sent a chill down Falken's spine. "You spilled your dinner."

He glanced down at himself. He was covered in the remnants of the meal Domlen had brought. He had no idea how to reply. He'd expected curses. Threats. Anything but that simple observation.

When Falken didn't answer, Lord Domlen narrowed his eyes. "Clean yourself. I'll get you more food. Do not hide by the door again or you will regret it." With that, he turned on his heel and left, slamming the heavy door and locking it behind him.

Falken sagged back against the floor, his body shaking from reaction. He felt as if he'd attempted to swim a flood-swollen river and had bounced off a few of the rocks before going over a waterfall. To top it all off, his stomach grumbled again.

He managed a smirk as he pushed himself to his feet and began to strip off his stained and wet clothing. He flung them on the floor and walked naked to the washbasin near the room's small mirror.

The heat from the fireplace kept him warm enough,

despite the damp and the cold rain outside. His mind was a tumble of thoughts and fears. He had a difficult time making sense of them. Why hadn't Domlen done anything more than fling him across the room—and that only when Falken had continued to attack him? Perhaps more punishment was coming. Or did his captor not want to damage a potential ransom?

Well, Falken wasn't about to argue with him there. Either way, it didn't matter. He would be able to take whatever the man dished out. He'd suffered through the torments of his older brothers, the "games" they had liked to play when they were young that often left Falken bleeding, bruised, and crying. He'd endured the rigorous training of the mind necessary to become a sorcerer. The long hours, the exhaustion, the grinding nights spent studying, and the constant demand for focus. He might not be as big or powerful as this Lord Domlen, but he was strong enough to face the man who had imprisoned him. He was strong enough to escape. This was only a small setback.

A grin turned up the corners of his lips. Yes, if his captor was reluctant to harm him even after Falken had tried to dash his brains in, then Domlen was nothing more than a toothless dragon. All roar, no bite. All smoke and no fire.

He was still rinsing his body with a wet cloth when the lock rattled again, meaning Domlen had returned with more food. Outside, the gloom had deepened. Now the glow of the few candles and the flames from the hearth bathed the tower room in warm light. This time, Domlen opened the door carefully and let it swing inward before he entered. He took a step inside, his gaze landing on Falken, and then he stopped dead.

Falken paused in the act of running the wet cloth up his

inner thigh, cleaning away the soup broth. Domlen's unusual reaction made him wonder if his captor intended to punish him after all. But Domlen was only staring at him...and something had changed. His gray eyes had lost that coldness they always held. As Falken stared back, he was both surprised and strangely gratified when Domlen's gaze trailed down the length of his body. Lingering like a visual caress...

What was this? The man couldn't be offended by his nudity. Or...surely Domlen could not be attracted to him...? Did Domlen love men the way Falken loved men? And why had his captor hidden it? Or, more precisely, why had the man not exploited it? Falken was helpless enough with the bracers on, suppressing his magic. Domlen had driven that point home easily enough. The lord of the fortress was large and heavily muscled. He could easily take whatever he wanted.

But there was no denying the flash of heat in the other man's eyes. Not fury. Not hatred. But lust. Desire.

Finally, Domlen looked away. He carried Falken's meal to the table and set it down. His jaw was clenched, his movements rigid. He appeared far more upset than he had after Falken had attacked him.

"Here is your dinner," Lord Domlen said, staring at the door instead of Falken. "I bid you a good evening."

"I'm not certain how it could be better," Falken replied, his tone dripping acid. "It never stops raining. The food is not worthy of maggots. And I'm a prisoner in your bloody tower."

Domlen still didn't look at him. He only nodded—nodding to the door instead of Falken, as though the door had been the one complaining—and then he left. His shoulders were so broad they nearly filled the doorway as he passed through. The sound of the key in the lock and his retreating footsteps told Falken he was alone at last.

He couldn't help but glance at the broken pieces of the bust lying on the floor as he padded across the room, still naked. Had he really believed he could kill the man with that? He needed something a whole lot bigger. Perhaps he could get Domlen to stand beneath a life-sized granite gargoyle and then hold still as Falken shoved it over onto him...

The meal was no surprise he discovered when he removed the cover. It was soupy, gritty concoction of grains, unidentifiable pickled vegetables, and chunks of salt mutton. The same as every meal. This place was truly hell. Rain that never ended, at best tapering off to a dreary drizzle. Abominable food. A huge and dangerous man who had kidnapped him from beneath the noses of the royal guard. His capture might not have had anything to do with the deadly, backstabbing politics of court or the treachery of Falken's older brothers, but that was little comfort. He'd take both of those possibilities in an instant if it meant being ransomed back to his father again, returning to the palace, and eating meals that didn't seem as if they'd been scraped from the bottom of someone's boot. Seeing the sun lifting for the dawn, or the moons traveling overhead, using magic again...

The need, the yearning to use magic pulled a groan of pure longing from deep inside him. If he had no other reason to hate Domlen, the man's choice to bar him from his magic was cause enough.

As he started to eat, a plan began to form in his mind. If he hadn't been mistaken and it *had* been a flash of desire in his captor's eyes, then that was something he could use at last. He might not be able to overpower the man without magic, but if he could seduce him… If he could tempt Lord Domlen into falling for him…

Well, that would change things completely. He grinned without humor as he spooned in the lukewarm slop. That sealed it. He would seduce his cold-hearted captor, no matter what he had to do, no matter what it might cost him. Lure him, entice him, persuade him to trust. And then, when Lord Domlen least expected it, Falken would let the jaws of the trap spring closed and he'd escape this horrible place forever.

* * *

Lord Domlen shoved through the large double doors leading into the fortress's main keep. Rainwater streamed off his cloak and dripped on the floor. He turned back and grabbed the doors, meaning to slam them shut again against the wet night. But his gaze fell upon the tower he'd just left, and he stopped.

Against the gloom of the storm clouds, the tower was a dark gray-green column, its sides streaked with mildew and moss. The burnished metal plates that adorned the surface had once reflected sunlight so brightly that the tower could be seen for miles, flashing like a beacon. It was so brilliant that, on some summer days, those working and selling in the courtyard had to raise pavilions and screens to shade themselves from the glare. This place had been known as the Fortress of the Sun, in part because of that tower, in part because of the spells that had once protected its walls. The curse of these unending storms had changed things years ago. Now it was known as the Fortress of Rain.

He stared at the dreary and green-streaked tower and wondered what Falken was doing right now, there in the highest room a hundred or more paces above the courtyard. Then, disgusted with himself, he slammed both doors shut with a resounding boom.

His boots left a trail of wet footprints behind on the flagstones as he walked, leaning forward as if charging into battle. His fists were clenched. His jaw was clenched. He wanted to break everything around him.

What had taken place inside the tower this evening should never have happened. Not Falken trying to ambush him — that was expected — but Domlen's reaction to the other man when he'd been...unclothed. He could not allow himself to...to *feel*...anything for the prince. That was dangerous to them all. Prince Falken was only a means to an end. He was nothing more than a tool Domlen intended to use to break something that had tormented his people for years.

But the sight of Prince Falken's naked body had stirred up feelings he believed he'd frozen out of himself long ago. He would not lie. Falken was desirable. His body was lean but well proportioned, his face comely, his cock beautifully shaped, dangling between his muscled thighs, his buttocks firm and tight. As he'd been staring at the man, Domlen's hand had twitched, yearning to reach out and touch the man's flesh. Caress him —

No. This could not be. He felt his lips curl into a snarl as he shoved through another set of doors, making his way along the corridors of the fortress. The lamps flickered with the breeze of his quick movement, making the flames flutter and jump. He did not slow. He felt as though he needed to burn off some of this mad energy sizzling inside him or he would burst into flames.

To say he was troubled by his reaction to his prisoner's body and disturbed by how readily his cock stirred to life at the sight of Falken nude would be an understatement. It was not a matter of Domlen's desire for men over women. He'd embraced that part of himself when he'd been young and had always been at peace with it. No, this was very different.

Absolutely nothing good could come of any attraction to the prince.

In seven days, on the night when the blood moon reigned unchallenged in the sky, he would take Prince Falken up onto the roof of the tower. There, in the rain and under the storm clouds, he would attempt a very difficult, very costly magic ritual.

That ritual would cost Prince Falken his life.

The ceremony was why Domlen had abducted the man and brought him to this godsforsaken place. Everything depended on it. It had taken him years of searching in distant lands after the books in the fortress's library had proven useless, many of them in languages he could not read. He'd always been a man of war, but desperation had turned him into a reluctant scholar. And to complete this horrible deed, he had to stay strong, had to harden his heart into unbreakable steel. Emotions had no place in him. Love had to be driven from his heart. They would only weaken his resolve.

He stormed through one of the outer halls. Mounted suits of empty armor stood sentry along the walls, as hollow inside as he felt right now. The large stone blocks making up the fortress walls were hung with ragged tapestries, some mildewed, others charred. Damage caused by the constant damp in the air or done during the siege of the fortress years ago. Much of the eastern curtain wall and the east fortress wing remained in ruins. That had been where the Boa Visk had finally breached the defenses. That had been the beginning of his failure as a leader.

"My lord," a woman's voice sounded behind him. The tone was hesitant, even tremulous, but also concerned. "My lord, are you well?"

He wheeled on her, his cloak flapping around him like wet sails and scattering droplets of water along the floor. The young woman drew back, startled. He immediately softened his expression, even contorting his face into what he hoped was a smile. It was Pilla. The serving girl he had surprised earlier in the courtyard when she'd been hiding in an alcove with her lover, Ronev, one of the fortress's guardsmen. She had large, pretty eyes the shade of bluebells, a heart-shaped face, and full lips. Yet, it was the warmth in her eyes that made her one of the most beloved of his servants by both women and men, highborn and low, from the captain of the guard to the steward to the stable hands. It was easy to understand what Ronev saw in her.

And it was bitterly tragic. So much so that every time he saw them together, it stabbed him like a knife in his heart.

He drew a deep breath and let it out slowly, mastering his emotions. He could not let his feelings rule him lest he slip and reveal the horrible truth to Pilla or Ronev or to any of the others inside the Fortress of Rain.

Carefully, he said, "I am fine, Pilla. Thank you for your concern." He lifted the edge of his drenched cloak, still pattering droplets on the floor. "Only a little damp tonight."

She grinned at him, and her face shone with good humor. "As you say, m'lord. You looked upset. Is it...?" She hesitated again, biting at her lip. Her skin color was healthy and vibrant. Much more so than his color was these days. Another bitter irony. "Is it the young lord who stays in the tower?"

His eyes narrowed. "Stay away from the tower."

She paled and bowed low. "Of course, m'lord. I don't go in the tower, as you commanded. I only wondered because you look unhappiest when you leave there. And the young lord looks awfully sad staring out the windows—"

"Perhaps you should focus more on dusting the halls and sweeping the floors," he said, hearing all the edges in his voice. "The tower is forbidden."

She bowed and practically fled from him. He watched her go, his heart sinking, and the old, tight ache in his chest returning with a vengeance. He had been too hard on her of course. She didn't understand. The girl had only been concerned for him, and he had treated her poorly, as he treated everyone poorly these days.

Yet, his command stood. He could not allow anyone into the tower. It was not a matter of secrecy—the prince was often at the two windows of his tower room, watching what happened below him in the fortress. Nor was it a matter of their safety, for Falken could not harm them. Domlen allowed no one inside the tower for a very simple reason.

Aside from the prince, Domlen was the only living person in this entire fortress of two hundred and seven souls.

All at once, he spun on his heel and delivered a smashing blow to the helmet of a nearby suit of armor. A terrific clamor rang out as armor pieces went flying in all directions. His fist had knocked the visored helm clean off the armor and spilled the entire suit to the floor. The echoes of clanging metal seemed to go on forever. His knuckles were raw and scraped, bleeding in places. He didn't feel it. He didn't care.

He stood there, staring down at the mess and feeling just as broken. The heavy burden of his position as lord of the fortress never gave him a moment's respite. Every day he was forced to live a lie, to hide a staggering truth, to take part in a mad charade.

Pilla and Ronev wanted to marry. They were in love. They'd been engaged to be wed before they'd been murdered.

It was the same for every person within the fortress, save himself. They'd all been executed when the defenses had failed and the Boa Visk—brutal, intelligent monsters with scaled, yellow-green skin—had taken the stronghold. Now they were all ghosts. Spirits of the dead. Their souls had been trapped here after the Boa Visk sorcerers cast the curse that turned the Fortress of the Sun into the Fortress of Rain. Each of them appeared alive, except for a few notable tells, mostly how their eyes would glow in low light and a certain coldness to their auras. Because of the curse and the power drawn from the blood moon, they were far more powerful than ordinary shades. They had form and could touch and affect the world around them. They retained their personalities, the hopes and dreams they'd had before their deaths. And each of them believed they still lived...except perhaps for the old scholar Yosel, who seemed to suspect something was badly wrong.

At first, Domlen had tried convincing the souls trapped here that they were no longer alive and needed to move on to find peace. But he'd quickly discovered that they could not move on to the afterlife, and even if he managed to make them see the truth, in a day's time the knowledge would leave them. It was frustrating beyond belief, and pushed him toward despair.

Still, the end result was the same. Now he took part in a daily charade where all the ghosts around him went about their duties and their lives in the fortress as if they still lived, and yet nothing ever changed. Pilla and Ronev never married.

Caramore, the head steward, was still overseeing the management of the fortress as if there were a garrison and a household to support. The phantom guards still walked the walls. Tommick, Domlen's captain of the guard, still made watch assignments and oversaw training. The lives of all his people remained in a cruel state of suspension. They were not really living, simply existing, unable to pass on to the afterlife where they could be happy.

He kicked aside a steel gauntlet from the suit of armor and continued down the hall toward his chambers. The guards he passed kept at attention, not wanting to draw his ire. They were good at sensing his dark moods. And there were many dark moods.

For a long time, he'd feared everyone in this fortress was trapped in this halfway existence forever. The Boa Visk used strange magics, dangerous and volatile. He'd been close to despair. On nights when he'd indulged in the wine cellar too heavily, he'd even considered taking his life, as weak and shameful as that seemed to him when sober and during the light of day. But at least he could truly join his people in their death.

When he'd had finally learned a way to break the curse, it had not freed him from despair. The needed ritual was obscure and costly, one that required blood from a member of a royal line. *All* the blood. In order to free his people from their nightmare, he would have to sacrifice an innocent man.

He would have to murder Prince Falken of Teirlan.

The heavy, iron-banded door to his chambers stood shut before him. He shouldered it open, letting it slam back into the wall. He lit one of the lamps and frowned at his disordered chambers, at the books strewn and stacked everywhere, his journals and research piled on the writing desk. The ink stains marring the wooden surface. The dirty bowls with remnants of the gruel he made from the remaining stores of food in the fortress, all he could prepare in a land where the sun never broke free of the clouds.

He leaned against the wall, suddenly feeling weak, his despair threatening to drown him. Because there was an even darker side to the curse created by the Boa Visk. More than the unending rains and the ghostly imprisonment of his people. That truth had set him on this path.

If he did not break this curse, one by one, his people would begin to change. They would lose their remaining humanity, all their love and compassion and kindness. The curse would transform them into revenir, phantoms ever hungry for the life force of the living. They were terrifying creatures. He'd heard tales of revenir plaguing the tundra of the Frost Isles, slaughtering every living creature and reducing the land to a frozen waste. If an army of revenir were loosed upon the unsuspecting lands surrounding the fortress, they would do untold damage and cost a great many lives.

He had already seen several disturbing signs among a few of the ghosts, hinting that for some, the change might be beginning. That only meant one thing.

He was running out of time.

CHAPTER TWO

The worst part of Falken's nightmare was that he knew full well he was dreaming and was still powerless to wake. This dream was like and yet unlike the day Domlen had captured him. Falken was walking through a forest, but instead of the tall trunks of evergreens and bright green ferns of the Daggerdown Woods, these trees were skeletal, pressed tightly together in a wall of entangled branches. He carried no weapon save a knife; he relied upon his magic when on the hunt for monsters. The magic surged and flared within him, as if his body contained fire inside instead of muscle and bone. He loved and missed the feeling.

Under orders from his father, he was tracking a jyrdoth drake rumored to be killing the livestock of borderland farmers. In the true world, the past world, he'd had the members of the royal bodyguard following behind him and moving along his flanks. In the dream, he was alone.

Darkness choked the forest around him. It was very quiet, so quiet that the sound of his breath rasped harshly in his ears.

Dread followed him with every step. Something was here with him, stalking him in the forest. Sometimes he saw its impossibly massive shadow pass over the trees and across the bloodred moon that peeked at him through the barren branches. He could hear it sometimes, rattling the dead strands of ivy and crushing branches. But whenever he turned in its direction, it was gone.

Fear took him. He began to run. Skeletal branches tore at him, scratched his face, but he didn't slow. The sound of booming footsteps and cracking tree limbs echoed behind him, growing closer. Closing in on him, not matter how hard he ran.

The forest became a blur around him, full of darkness and terror. The thing behind him was very close now, its shadow spread before it like a black wave. Falken stumbled into a clearing, praying that he was safe now that he'd escaped from the trees. Beyond the clearing rose a tall, dreary tower, streaked with moss and slime. It was the tower he'd been trapped inside since his capture.

His legs gave out. He stumbled to his knees, jolts of pain traveling up his hands into his wrists. A snapping and cracking sounded behind him as something huge and dark shouldered aside two trees blocking its path. The man-shape was massive, ten paces high at least, and wrapped in a purple-black cloak and hood that hid its face in shadow.

It began to rain. The dark giant reached for him. Falken couldn't move, not even when the hooded-figure's huge hand clamped down on his shoulder. He could only stare up into the inky blackness inside the hood as the dark shape drew a knife blade and lifted it high to plunge into his heart.

Overhead, the blood moon gleamed like the crimson eye of the jyrdoth drake he'd hunted but never found.

Falken jerked awake with a cry. Something had him by the shoulder, shaking him. He wrenched away, swinging at it. His hand smacked against something solid, knocking it aside. An instant later his eyes focused and his mind finally told him what he was seeing.

Lord Domlen sat beside him on the bed. Falken had smacked Domlen's hand away from where the man had been gripping his shoulder, shaking him awake. The terror from the dream still lingered in Falken's sweat. He flinched away from the other man, uttering a growl that sounded more like a groan of pain.

Domlen slowly withdrew his hand. There was a red mark on his skin where Falken had struck him. His mouth was tight, though his expression was emotionless. But those storm-cloud eyes of his were striking, and there was no mistaking the flash of pain in them, stark and clear to the world, before Domlen closed himself off again and those eyes went colder than the rain.

"You were having a nightmare," Domlen told him.

"Do not touch me," Falken said as he pushed himself to a sitting position on the bed. The sheets fell from his body to pool around his waist. He'd always slept naked, even before he'd set out to seduce this man, and now the bedsheets barely covered his lower half.

Set out to seduce the man. That had been his intention, but here he was knocking away Domlen's hand and snarling warnings at him. He'd seen Domlen's pain at the rejection, though he didn't understand it. Did the man honestly think Falken would ever be happy to see him? He hadn't begun his seduction game yet, so how could Domlen hope for anything but hatred and anger from a man he kept locked in a room that was nothing more than a lavishly furnished cell?

Regardless, antagonizing him would be moving in entirely the wrong direction. So Falken forced himself to take a deep breath and shake out the rest of the fear that had invaded his body and still lingered from the nightmare like clammy sweat. He tried on a smile, nothing too warm. Domlen was not a fool. He'd suspect what Falken was up to if he dropped all his hostility at once. This needed to be a gradual lure. This was tempting the predator into the trap.

"I'm sorry," Falken said, keeping brusqueness in his tone but softening it some. "The nightmare—" The blood moon. The tower. The chase by an enemy who couldn't be anyone else but Domlen. "My dreams were unsettling."

"I understand," came Domlen's simple reply.

Falken couldn't help but steal a glance at him. The other man's expression had turned grim, but his gaze remained steady. He had the sense that his captor, for whatever reason, truly did understand. Perhaps his guilt at keeping Falken prisoner weighed upon his dreams in the dark hours of the night. Or perhaps he was guilty of even worse things.

The reasons didn't matter. What mattered was that Domlen had surprised him awake and his strategy had gotten off to a rocky start. All his life he'd had issues with speaking before his mind could carefully consider the words escaping his mouth. The flaw had landed him in no end of trouble with his father, his brothers, and members of the court. "Don't touch me," was not how one went about a successful seduction.

That misstep aside, it was time to begin luring the man in, and what better way than with lust? He shifted his position on the bed, allowing the sheets to fall farther away from his body. Now they were barely covering the dark thatch of hair at his groin, leaving part of his hip and buttocks exposed. He noticed Domlen's jaw briefly tighten, but the man kept his gaze focused on Falken's face.

Well, there was still time to add to the bait. He gave a languid stretch and a yawn as he glanced about the room. He could smell food, but even though his breakfast was covered by a serving tray, he realized it was the same scent as usual. The same bland gruel.

The realization suddenly sparked him to anger. "Would it kill you to feed me something else for once? Even a stale hunk of bread would be better than the same thing, morning, noon, and night."

He clamped his jaws shut before he could say anything further. Damn his tongue. Perhaps this wouldn't be as easy as he'd believed, especially if he couldn't control his mouth.

Domlen stood and moved to the fireplace with a heavy tread. The big man certainly had an undeniable presence. The way a dangerous bear had a presence. He squatted and began to arrange pieces of split wood on the iron grate. Falken figured the man planned on ignoring his comment about the food until Domlen suddenly rumbled a reply in his rough, deep voice. "There is no other food. We are lucky to have it. And lucky to have salt and vinegar to preserve the mutton and the vegetables."

"Lucky" wasn't how Falken would describe it. These meals were the poorest fare he'd ever eaten. They were far worse than his time spent on the hunt been on the hunt or on the annual three-month-long trek when his father sent him to the distant forts and strongholds of Teirlan to collect taxes and reinforce the power of the throne.

All the same, this was the most Domlen had said to him

in days. It had to be a result of all the skin he was showing. He suppressed a grin and decided to push his advantage. He slid out of bed and made his way naked to the washbasin and the pitcher of water there.

"I suppose sheep are common to a place such as this," he said easily. "A place lost to the sun and drowning in rain. What gods did your land anger to end up so cursed?"

Domlen stopped in the act of striking flint against the steel he'd taken from the mantle. He didn't speak, although his body radiated a coiled tension. Instead, he struck the flint and steel together hard, sending a flash of sparks onto the tinder. Then he gently blew on the sparks until the tinder caught and the flames spread to the kindling.

His captor was no longer looking Falken's way, which meant his wandering around nude was wasted on them man...although the tension in the air had definitely increased. So perhaps Domlen was struggling with himself not to peek. Silently, he urged the man to stare, to drink the sight in, for his cock to get hard and make the man foolish and reckless, the way all men with hard cocks always were.

Instead, Domlen continued to stare at the flickering yellow flames eating at the kindling. He surprised Falken by speaking, though his voice was quiet and soft. "Have you never heard of this place, then?"

Falken turned to him, frowning. Could Domlen be foolish enough to tell him where he was trapped? His captor had never given any details or hints. His accent was from the north, but how far from Teirlan had the man taken him? Falken didn't recognize the fortress or its surroundings, but he was certainly interested in knowing...so he could be at the head of his father's army when he attacked and razed it.

But what he said aloud was, "*Should* I have heard of it?"

Domlen turned to look him straight in the eye. There was no flick of his gaze down to Falken's exposed manhood, none of the desire of yesterday. His stare bored directly into Falken's eyes. "This is the Fortress of Rain."

His captor spoke as if the name should mean something to him. Falken only shook his head slowly. The name did stir something far back in his memory, some rumor, some distant myth, not an old one either. It irritated him, for he felt as if he should know it. But his mind was mostly filled with spell lore and magic, that and information he needed to navigate his way through the rocky shoals of the Lindermain court. The Fortress of Rain was an apt title, but it certainly was no stronghold inside Teirlan or he would know of it.

For a moment it looked as if Domlen might just smile. That was something Falken had never witnessed. But instead, he only adjusted the log with the iron tongs. His voice, when he spoke again, sounded wistful and tinged with sadness. "Perhaps you know it by another name. Solarahold, the Fortress of the Sun. On clear days, your tower would reflect the sunlight from the spell-protected metal fused to the stonework. The tower became a brilliant beacon for leagues, resembling a pillar of light."

Falken chose to ignore the words "your tower," because if he didn't, he might just attack Domlen with another heavy object. As for hearing of this Solarahold...again it sounded vaguely familiar, like the name of some city in a legend.

"I'm sorry," he said with a frown. "Perhaps this Solarahold was not as famous as you believed." He walked to his clothing, all provided by Domlen of course, and began to yank it on, more than a little irked his nudity wasn't having the expected effect on the other man. "I can see why they changed the name. Does this cursed, rain-soaked swamp *ever* see a clear day? It's enough to make a man want to drown his sorrow, or maybe himself, in a cask of ale."

Domlen did not reply. Instead, he stood and headed straight for the door.

Fear raced through the prince. Clearly his words had offended the man. In order to have any chance with this scheme to seduce Domlen, Falken needed as much time with the man as he could manage. His captor was quiet and brooding enough as it was, and now Falken's cursed tongue wasn't helping the matter. If Domlen left now, the prince would be alone until Domlen returned with his evening meal.

"Forgive me," he said quickly, though it galled him to the bone. "I'm still out of sorts from the nightmare." Relief swept through him when Domlen stopped, though he did not turn around again. So Falken continued, because the subject seemed important to Domlen and he was eager to hook the man back in. "I have not heard of any Fortress of the Sun or Rain. I'd like to hear the tale, if you'll tell it."

At first, he believed the lord would leave anyway. But after a long pause, Domlen turned to look at him again. "The Boa Visk attacked here, a long time ago."

Falken nodded and his sudden flash of sympathy didn't need to be acted. The Boa Visk were a truly monstrous scourge, with powerful, strange magic. They were as intelligent as any human, with a poisonous bite and scaled, yellow-green skin. Their orange eyes gleamed in the dark. When Falken had been a boy, his kingdom of Teirlan had been at war all along their borders with the Boa Visk-controlled kingdom of Tyrdevna. But years ago, generals in Tyrdevna began to turn the tide of the war in their favor within the kingdom's borders, which had taken the pressure off Teirlan. He'd heard plenty of tales of Boa Visk brutalities that turned the stomach and chilled the heart.

He ventured a careful reply, knowing this was dangerous ground. "It seems as though your fortress held strong if it still stands and the people are safe."

Again that twist came to the other man's face, almost a smile, but this time the expression was deeply bitter. "As my grandsire often said, 'Appearances can be deceiving.'"

Deceiving or not, it seemed as though there would be no more forthcoming details from his captor after that single cryptic statement. Falken had to swallow his frustration. The man had the conversational skills of a dead tree. But now Falken was dressed, and his stomach was rumbling, despite the food being foul swill he'd feel guilty forcing upon a pig.

He sat at the table pushed against the gently curved wall of heavy stone blocks and removed the lid from the serving dish. He was not surprised to find the exact same meal he'd eaten every day here since his arrival. Instead of dwelling on it, he began to spoon the salty muck into his mouth.

He noticed Domlen watching him again. It seemed the man didn't have a problem looking Falken's way when he was clothed. Interesting. There had to be a way for him to twist that to his advantage.

"So," Falken said, grasping about for a topic of conversation to keep the man here longer. He needed more time so he could continue working on him. But he had to be careful of what he said, never his strong suit. He settled on something he considered safe enough. "The serving girl and her guardsman lover that I see constantly sneaking off to indulge their mutual feelings... What are their names?"

Lord Domlen tensed, his eyes narrowing dangerously as his hands bunched into fists. In Falken's mind, the memory of the dream monster chasing him through the forest flashed back into his thoughts.

Unnerved, he continued quickly, wondering what he'd said wrong while nonchalantly trying to play it off. "I often see them from my windows. They slink around as if their love is forbidden and they must keep it hidden, but from what I could tell, every person in the fortress is aware of it." He tried out a laugh, but Domlen didn't join him, and it sounded awkward and forced. "It's very…" He paused, fumbling for the word with the right shade of meaning until he finally had it. "Endearing."

"They are none of your concern. Do not speak to them. Do not try to catch their attention. If you will not obey, I will block up these windows. Or perhaps you would prefer a cell in the dungeon?"

Falken set his spoon down and narrowed his eyes. Only his father and his brothers ever spoke to him so imperiously. As if this minor lordling of some obscure, waterlogged fort had the right to threaten *him*.

"And what else am I supposed to do?" he demanded, rising from his seat and facing off against the other man. "I'm a prisoner here, damn you. It's long past time I learned what you wanted and who paid you to kidnap me. Was it one of my brothers?" He laughed without humor. "My brothers would sooner cut your throat than pay you whatever they promised."

"Do not talk to anyone here but me," Lord Domlen repeated, dismissing every word he'd said.

"As if there is any chance of that." Falken wanted to sweep the remaining food off the table in a gesture of defiance but held himself back. True, the food was always borderline inedible, but he was famished, and the action only seemed juvenile and petulant. He'd much rather take one of the logs from the fire and bash the other man with it. "You're going to pay for keeping me here. What ransom did you set? I hope it is worth your life."

"No ransom," Domlen said coldly. "We are a thousand leagues from Teirlan. They will never search for you here, in a place that is curse-bound and shunned. The peasants fear this place, and you should as well. Now keep your clothes on in my presence, and give up your childish dreams of freedom. You are here forever."

* * *

Lord Domlen raised the axe overhead in a smooth arc. Then he put all his strength into bringing the axe down on the length of wood he'd balanced on the oak stump he was using as a cutting block. The axe blade sheared through the wood and sent the two pieces toppling off the block into the mud. He snatched up the pieces, scraped off the mud, and tossed them beneath a large oilskin tarp to keep them dry. Or at least in an attempt to keep them dry.

The rain felt icy on his body. He'd stripped down to his breeches, and water vapor steamed on his hot skin. He snatched up another piece of wood. Set it on the block. Brought the axe down again. He repeated this over and over again. His axe-blows struck with precision every time. Most swings hit so hard the blade not only split the log but drove deep into the cutting block. By now he had more than enough wood for both his and Falken's needs, but he didn't stop. He wouldn't stop until he was exhausted. He'd cut wood until he purged all his fury and all the desire out of his system. Until he was empty again.

He began chopping faster and faster. His muscles burned and ached, but he didn't relent. He heard himself grunting like an animal as he drove the axe blade down, relishing the shudder of impact up through the shaft, up his forearms, into his shoulders. When he was out of wood, he hacked the tree stump to kindling. Finally, there was finally nothing left to cut.

Domlen stood there, head down, leaning on the axe haft, breathing hard. Water and sweat ran down his face and neck, down his bare chest, and soaked his breeches. His skin felt as if it were on fire. His muscles trembled with strain.

He needed to get control of himself. His emotions were running wild. These urges would destroy everything if he left them unchecked. Interacting with Falken was making him weak, leaving him vulnerable. Earlier, a small, traitorous part of his mind had even entertained the idea of not sacrificing Falken to complete the ritual. Of again trying to discover another way to break the curse…or finding someone else to sacrifice in his place.

But that part of him had been weak. It was only loneliness and selfishness that made his heart ache this way. As lord of this fortress, it would be the height of dishonor to deny his responsibilities to his people or his duty to end their suffering. Or to deny his obligations to the innocent people beyond the borders of the curse who would be attacked when the docile ghosts inside the fortress finally turned into revenir. He was being selfish, tempted by his own needs, his own isolation and pain, and he hated himself for it.

The blood moon night was again approaching. During the blood moon, the crimson-colored Vosk would be at its fullest and the only moon in the sky, its sister moons all dark. Then he would be forced to perform the ritual to end the curse. He had no other choice.

The rain had intensified. He'd been too far lost in his grim thoughts and hadn't noticed. Not only had the rain turned to a downpour, but the wind was steadily picking up in intensity. The clouds overhead were darker and more ominous than usual. As he peered up at them through the sheets of rain, he noticed their movement across the sky seemed to hold to a broad circular pattern, and a chill went through him. He'd seen the pattern before, almost always before a rage storm hit. These rage storms were rare but frightening in their intensity. He'd better hurry back inside before the storm reached its full strength.

He quickly shrugged back into his tunic and cloak, wincing as the soaking wet cloth stuck to his body. Then he began to stack the wood he'd chopped onto a sledge to take it back inside before the storm grew any worse. He glanced at the men on the battlements, picking them out through a sheet of misty-spray as the hard rain bounced back from the stone. The storms couldn't affect them, although oftentimes the ghosts behaved as if they did. Memories. He sometimes wondered what it was like for the spirits trapped here. Whether they understood something was terribly wrong. On occasion he had even asked, but the spirits always seemed confused and disbelieving. If he ever got them to admit something was wrong, they quickly forgot about it again. It was as though their minds could not conceive that they were dead but had been trapped here, denied the true afterlife and cursed to this half life.

Lightning flashed across the sky, followed by thunder so loud it seemed to shake the earth beneath his boots. The rain was driving down harder, pushed at an angle by the force of the wind. He hauled the sledge along the flagstones and through the spiderweb streams of water all running toward the drains. Outside the fortress, the moats would be cresting fast and the drainage channels near overflowing. Likely the nearby Loredine River would soon top its banks. Yet, this wouldn't be their first flood, and likely not their last.

Unless he performed the ritual under the crimson moon.

He glanced at the tower again. It was the tallest structure of the fortress, the top battlement used as a lookout for enemy armies approaching through the Koltero Mountains or from the Green Valley Plains to the south. He'd stood up there himself and watched as the Boa Visk army had advanced out of the mountain passes. He vividly remembered the fear he'd felt back then, knowing these vile creatures who had conquered so much of the world were now gathering to attack the Fortress of the Sun. He'd sent riders and lit the watch fires, calling for aid. No one had come. Then the siege had begun in earnest.

But Prince Falken wouldn't care about that. The man had never heard of the Fortress of the Sun or the thing it had become after the curse: the haunted Fortress of Rain, shunned by all living creatures. Either Teirlan was too distant for the story to have widely spread, or Falken had dismissed the tale as a fable used to scare children into being good and had forgotten it. Either way, it bothered him that Falken had no idea what this place was or what his people had suffer. What they were still suffering.

The wind pushed harder at his back. Quickly, he wiped the rain out of his eyes, looking up at the glow of candlelight in Falken's window. Despite himself, he wondered what the other man was doing now. It was disturbingly easy to imagine the other man's large, soulful eyes. Those eyes seemed to dominate his delicate features. The look in those eyes was often distrustful, wary, many times angry. But other times Domlen would catch a glimpse of what the young man had been like before he had abducted the prince from his homeland and imprisoned him here. So alive, vibrant, full of strength and lust and energy. Speaking his mind with nary a care. Ready to conquer the world. Domlen's heart lusted for that simplicity, that vibrancy, hope, and life, even more than he lusted for the other man's body —

He shoved those thoughts aside, damning himself again for his selfishness, for yearning for happiness when there was so much at stake. He had to remember, all that was left to him now was duty and pain...and staining his heart with murder to set his people free. He couldn't afford to lose sight of that.

As he turned and began to trudge back to the main keep, the rage storm finally broke overhead. The wind ramped up into a howling scream, strong enough to send him staggering as it whipped the folds of his cloak about him. The impact of each raindrop felt like being pelted with gravel. The chill in the air had deepened. Overhead, the clouds were churning ominously, and forks of lightning crisscrossed the sky or stabbed down at the dark mountain range around them.

He pulled his hood down lower, gritted his teeth, and pressed on. The lightning lit the fortress in brilliant blue-white flashes. The thunder boomed and echoed. He'd nearly made it to the main keep when a stroke of lightning pierced down and struck the top of Falken's tower. The nearly instantaneous crash of thunder had his ears ringing. Then another bolt flashed and struck the tower. Before the crack-rumble of thunder had even begun to fade, a *third* lightning bolt cut through the air and hit the tower's parapet. After the blazing afterimages of the lightning strikes began to fade from his eyes, he noticed the candlelight glow he could normally see shining through the tower shutters of Falken's room was no longer there.

Dread ripped through him with the force of the howling wind. Had something happened to Falken when the lightning hit the tower? It was far from the first time the tower had been struck, but why had the candles gone out?

He started toward the tower entrance, walking quickly at first then breaking into a flat out run. His boots skidded on the wet flagstones and he fell. He was up again in an instant, his knees and palms stinging, soaked now from both the rain and the puddles. But he didn't care about the chill or the wet. He had to see if Falken was safe. The ghosts of guards and servants silently watched him from the safety of other towers, windows, and covered battlements, but he ignored them. One of the guards seemed to be moving in his direction through the sheets of rain, calling something to him. Domlen couldn't tell who it was and had no patience to wait and see.

He shouldered through the thick double doors at the base of the tower. By his strict orders, there were no guards or servants inside the tower. He didn't want to risk Falken learning the truth about the curse on the fortress.

The stone stairs wound their way up the tower in a series of landings that led to other rooms. He was breathing hard by the time he reached the third landing. Now he regretted pushing himself so hard when he'd been cutting wood. Still, he ran on, taking the steps two at a time until he reached the topmost landing. From here, one set of stairs led to the tower's rooftop battlements, and opposite those stairs was the door to Falken's room. He fumbled the key out from his pocket. His hands were shaking so badly that he nearly dropped it twice. Finally, he had the door unlocked and he shoved it inward.

Falken stood at the east-facing window with the shutters thrown open. He'd been looking out at the storm, but he turned when Domlen burst into the room. The candles were all out, and the only light came from the low flames at the hearth and the flashes of lightning.

A wry smile turned up the prince's lips. "Forget something, Lord Domlen?"

"Are you safe?"

"Safe from the gods trying to hit me with lightning?" He spread his hands and looked down at his body. Then he made a show of dusting off his tunic and gray breeches. "As you can see, I'm not even wet." His eyebrows lifted and his expression was curious. "Although I do thank you for your concern."

Outside, the wind howled and pushed at the closed shutters of the other window, rattling them as if something were trying to get inside. The roar of the rain on the battlements overhead was loud enough that they were forced to raise their voices to be heard. All the while, the rapid flashes of lightning continued unabated.

Domlen moved farther inside and slowly peered around the prince's room. The fire in the hearth had burned low, but the candles were all out, which was why he hadn't seen their glow from the courtyard.

"Why are there no candles?" he demanded, the change from fear to relief making his tone harsh. Although he was weak with relief that no harm had come to Falken, he was also annoyed that he'd run up the tower steps and made a spectacle of himself for no apparent reason.

Falken leaned against the wall near the window and crossed his arms, eyeing him. "The wind blew them out with a big gust. Quite a storm. You look like you were out swimming in it."

Domlen gritted his teeth, not wanting to explain how he'd been out cutting wood…hacking logs into small chunks just to force the thoughts of Falken out of his mind for a little while.

A huge gust of wind roared against the stone and metal sides. The tower actually felt as if it swayed a little—an ominous sensation. Another rapid series of lightning strikes flashed outside, so bright and so quick that for a moment it seemed as if it were high noon inside the tower room.

"I suppose…I'll wish you a good-night then," Domlen said, gritting his teeth at how awkward and uncertain he sounded.

"You could stay and I could try and hit you with another statue." Falken pointed to the last bust in the room, a small one portraying the features of Jondain, the god said to have brought magic to humankind. "I wouldn't mind breaking that one over your head, if you're game. I always thought the Jondain myth to be patronizing beyond belief." He shrugged. "Or you can throw me around a little more, if that's more to your taste."

"I don't find your jests amusing."

"What can I say to that?" He held out his hands, showing the crovmane bracers that Domlen had sealed around his wrists, neutering his power. "Being cut off from the source of my magic makes me snide."

He was about to reply when someone spoke from behind him, making him flinch and wheel around.

"M'lord, is all well here?" Ronev asked. "Do you need assistance?"

Domlen stared at Ronev, the guardsman who was Pilla the serving girl's lover. She had been set to marry him for years and years now, the ceremony never reaching completion because the two of them were dead and trapped in an existence that did not change. The young guard must have seen him running toward the tower and followed him. Like a fool, Domlen had failed to shut and lock the door behind him. Now one of the fortress's ghosts was in the room with the very man he wanted to keep as far away from them as possible.

"Everything is well, Ronev," he said quickly, trying to will his heartbeat to slow to a normal pace again. Trying to keep his expression blank, as though there was nothing here that might spark Falken's suspicions. "Please leave us."

Ronev glanced at Prince Falken before bowing and retreating. Domlen shut the door and locked it. He stood there, breathing hard, water dripping off him and puddling on the floor, desperate to think of something to say and failing. He slowly turned back to Falken.

The prince was staring at the door, not moving, his face occasionally lit by flashes of lightning. Then he turned his gaze back to Domlen. His expression was stricken and pale.

It was clear Falken had noticed something was wrong with Ronev. From afar, the ghosts could not easily be distinguished from the living. Up close, they seemed to shimmer with a slight unearthly light. Their eyes had a soft glow to them, both brighter and yet less focused than those of the living. It was rare, but on occasion the illusion or magic making them seem solid grew weaker and parts of the wall or their surroundings became visible through their bodies. Despite the darkness of the storm, Falken might have noticed any of these things.

"He is dead," Falken finally said, his tone flat.

"That's a mad thing to say," Domlen replied, taking a

gamble on diverting the other man's suspicions with a show of scorn. "You're either storm blinded or drunk."

As he spoke, another round of thunder shook the tower and the wind howls increased, then died off, increased and faded again. The prince's expression turned from one of shock to one of anger.

"Don't lie to me. I've studied at the Vadolcadium in Lindermain. The sorcerers there are among the best in all the lands, and there are powerful necromancers as well. I've seen ghosts, spoken with spirits. I've even summoned a phantom as part of my studies. That guardsman was not alive."

Domlen could only stare at the prince. No words would come to him. Not even the simplest lie. He should've had some elaborate story prepared in the event that this ever happened. But it wasn't *supposed* to happen. He'd been so careful to keep the prince isolated. Now Falken knew. And if he didn't know the entire truth, it wouldn't take him long to either uncover it or invent some mad story to explain it.

"Is he the only one?" Falken pressed.

Domlen did not answer. He turned away, feeling as though he were fleeing from the prince. The wind gusted, battering the shutters again. He grabbed the door, intending to shut it. To stop the questions.

Falken hurried across the room toward him. "Is that why you brought me here? I am no necromancer. I have little skill with the dead. I cannot help you."

Domlen didn't dare reply. He retreated into the gloom of the landing and pulled the door shut behind him. As he locked it, Falken begin to yell from the other side of the door.

"What kind of demon-bastard are you? I *won't* help you. May the gods damn you if you killed that man and bound him here. Are you planning on doing the same to me?"

Domlen stood just outside the door, his hands shaking as emotions raged through him. Hot tears spilled from his eyes, and he was helpless to stop them or to hide his shame. He cursed his weakness, cursed himself for how his iron control had slipped. But he didn't make a sound, didn't utter a sob. Instead, he slammed his fist into the center of the door so hard that his knuckles left sharp indentations and the tower echoed with the boom. There was a startled gasp from the other side of the door, and then silence.

Domlen stared at the dents his knuckles had left in the wood. Then he turned on his heel, descended the long flight of stairs, and headed back into the storm. His blow to the door hadn't released the pressure building inside him and hadn't made him feel the least bit better.

Then again, nothing did these days.

CHAPTER THREE

After Domlen gave no answers and slammed the door, at first Falken could only panic. He ran to the door and tried the handle, but of course it was locked. Then he threw more wood on the fire and lit every candle and lamp in the room, as if the light could protect him from the spirits of the dead. His thoughts fluttered around helplessly in his mind like trapped birds. He couldn't sit still. He paced around the room as the storm raged and howled outside the tower.

What in the name of the gods had he been dragged into here? At first it had been easy to believe he'd been captured by a bandit or a rebel lord hoping to ransom him. It had hurt his pride, true, but he'd been forced to admit that Domlen had ambushed him and taken him down, despite the fact that Falken had been on the hunt for a drake and despite the royal guard charged with keeping him safe.

Much later, after the long ride to this isolated fortress while tied up and gagged in the back of a wagon, he'd started to suspect that his brothers had played some role in this kidnapping. Perhaps they needed him out of the way for one of the dozen plots and intrigues they always had going at once. He tried to stay out of the disgusting quagmire of court politics, but it was hardly possible when you were one of the king's three sons. Power and intrigue simply followed you everywhere.

Because Domlen had nullified his magic with these cursed bracers, it stood to reason that someone who knew Falken was involved in the abduction, possibly even someone from the Vadolcadium. The man had simply been too prepared. Someone must have informed him of Falken's spell talents and divulged where he'd be so Domlen could plan his strike. In the beginning, he'd tried making deals with Domlen. Then he'd tried threats. Bribes. Pleading. Nothing worked. Domlen was as cold and impassive as one of the gargoyles on the fortress towers.

Now he began to fear there was something far deeper and darker involved that he did not understand. And because he didn't understand it, the whole thing loomed large in his mind, crushing his ability to think with the panic caused by its shadow. It was as if he were trapped in the nightmare again—the forest and the tower, being chased by the demon who went by the name of Lord Domlen.

The guard had been a phantom spirit. Oh, he'd been one of the most lifelike ghosts Falken had ever seen, but there was no mistaking that unnatural glow, the presence that seemed to suck the heat out of the living, or those eyes shimmering with their own light. If the guard was a spirit, that meant the serving girl was a ghost as well. Which begged the question:

how many of the people in this fortress were alive and how many were the phantom undead?

The only person he was certain was truly alive was Lord Domlen. He had no idea what had happened at this borderland fortress, save what little Domlen had seen fit to tell him. The dreaded Boa Visk had been involved. That could mean anything. But he'd seen no evidence of a Boa Visk garrison here, and he assumed that if they'd taken the fortress and still held it, he'd have spotted one of them by now through the windows. There was no mistaking the reptilian creatures, their strange clothes, or their disconcerting eyes.

The thunder was now coming at longer and longer intervals. The storm was finally dying out. He walked to the open window and put his hands on the rain-soaked ledge. So many things didn't make sense. He was grasping at a shape in the dark, trying to tell what it was but with too little information. For example, Domlen hadn't thrown him in the dungeon. He'd assumed it was because he rated as a valuable, highborn prisoner to ransom. It was hard to collect a ransom if the noble prisoner died of wet lung in a dungeon before the money was paid. Although with this constant rain, one could just as easily die of wet lung in an exquisite tower room as die of it in a damp dungeon.

The rain. He stared out at the rain lashing the battlements and the courtyard. Of course he'd wondered over the rain. It was unnatural to never see the sun. But what if this were all somehow connected? These unending storms and the ghosts who didn't seem to know they were ghosts. He shook his head. Right now, he had no idea what the common thread between them could be. All the evidence seemed random and disconnected. Storms. Phantoms. A noble lord who had traveled hundreds of leagues or more to capture the third son of a king in a land that Falken suspected didn't even border this one.

He watched as the clouds overhead slowed their churning and the lightning moved to the horizon to flash over the dark shapes of the mountains. He held his hand out and stared at the rain that dotted his skin and began to pool in his palm.

Why did Domlen want him?

Frustrated, he clenched his fist and pulled the shutters closed. He went to the hearth and squatted before it, watching the water drip from his hands and hiss on the hot stone. His thoughts raced faster than wild horses and were just as uncontrollable. He kept thinking about the hurt he'd glimpsed in Domlen's eyes when his mask slipped. Perhaps there was far more to the man than the demon Falken had believed him to be. What were the secrets he held? It was abundantly clear from the man's dismayed expression that he hadn't expected the ghost to follow him into the tower. Had Domlen killed all the people here and bound them to him as spirit servants? Was he a necromancer of some kind? Again, if that were so, why would Domlen capture him? The man seemed to have no talent for magic. Either that or he hid his talent extremely well. He was a warrior lord. So there wasn't anything Falken could teach him…

Was he lonely? Falken shook his head in contempt at the thought, but then he forced himself to consider it. Stranger things had happened. Falken had believed *he'd* been the one trying to seduce Domlen, to bend him to his will, but what if the entire time it had been the other way around? What if Domlen was wearing him down, making him submissive, dependent, desperate. Turning him into…what? Some kind of love slave? It was absurd.

But now that he considered it, there was a deep shadow

on the man. A sorrow and a weight he'd chosen to hide behind his gruff and imperious facade. But the moment Domlen had been staring at Falken when he'd been naked and cleaning himself, there had been real yearning in his eyes. Desire, lust, yes there had been both, but underpinning them had been that longing for touch, for connection.

If Lord Domlen was the only living soul in a fortress full of ghosts, it was no wonder he felt that way. In truth, it was a miracle the man had not gone mad.

Now all that was left was for Falken to discover a way to unravel this dark mystery completely so he could use that knowledge to escape and leave this tower of insanity behind him forever.

CHAPTER FOUR

"Tonight is the blood moon," Lord Domlen said.

Falken slowly set down his spoon, leaving the last chunk of grayish salt-mutton untouched. He turned to look at the other man as his heart lurched in his chest. He'd suspected something bad was about to happen from the moment Domlen had unlocked the tower door. For the first time since Domlen had captured him, he'd arrived wearing a long knife on his belt secured in a leather sheath. Falken had pretended not to notice, but his stomach had been all twisted up with dread the entire time he'd been eating. It was difficult enough to choke down these meals without the man who'd captured him brooding in the corner of the room while wearing a blade.

"The blood moon, you way? I wasn't aware." He jerked his chin at the bookshelves stacked with leather-bound volumes. Unfortunately, there were no spell grimoires or treatises on magic, but there were a fair amount of books on history and myth. A few good plays from Arnoth, known for its dramas. There had even been one naughty little book he'd discovered — a tale full of action and sex, telling the lurid story of a sea captain who fell in love with his first mate as they hunted a sea monster. That one had provided the most entertainment yet. "There were no almanacs on the shelves," he continued, sitting up straighter in his chair. "So what significance does the crimson moon have? We can't even see it with the rain clouds."

His words came out smoothly and full of practiced nonchalance. He was praying the announcement was just a passing bit of conversation from the man, nothing relevant. Simply a casual observation. Because Falken knew what significance the blood moon had for magic and spell craft. There were plenty of powerful and dangerous spells that could only be fully empowered on a blood moon, when Vosk waned and dominated the night sky. That was when ghost could more easily cross the veil between the living and the dead, and spirit summoning grew far more powerful.

But Domlen was no necromancer, no sorcerer. What could the blood moon mean to him? Falken had an uneasy feeling that it had something to do with the ghosts. And why did the man need that damned knife? It gave off an aura of power easy enough to sense even with the cursed bracers walling him off from using his magic.

"I'm sorry I don't have better fare for you," Domlen said, glancing at the gray-green soup in Falken's bowl along with a burned chunk of bread as tough as leather. This was, in fact, the first time he'd been served bread, which meant Domlen had probably baked it himself, for a reason. "I was never skilled at making bread."

"That explains why the food is terrible," he replied, using a jape to hide his growing disquiet. "Phantoms are indifferent cooks."

Did the man almost smile at his jest? He couldn't tell. But he had the uneasy feeling that it was too late. If Falken hadn't broken through Domlen's cold, iron shell by now, there was little hope.

He'd utterly failed to seduce Domlen in the days following the rage storm and the lightning strikes. Perhaps that had been a ludicrous plan from the beginning. But after Falken had discovered the truth about the ghosts, Domlen had withdrawn further into his icy shell. He delivered the meals and left. If Falken happened to be sleeping late and naked, Domlen still did not linger, did not even glance his way. He barely spoke, and he certainly did not respond to any of Falken's questions.

As the days had passed, Falken had never felt more isolated, more alone. He spent his time reading or watching the few servants and guards he could see from his windows, looking for tells that they were phantoms. Now that he knew what he was looking for, he did seem to catch them involved in odd behaviors. They stopped and stared off into space. Sometimes they seemed to wander aimlessly, then would come back to themselves and hurry away. Occasionally one would wander behind a tower on the outer wall, leaving his line of sight...and never appear on the other side. Strange things, most of them minor and difficult to notice if one wasn't paying close attention. Yet he had little else to do but ponder this disturbing mystery.

The morning after the storm, he did not see Lord Domlen at all. Later that evening, when Domlen finally brought his meal, the man had refused to answer any of Falken's questions and had given only cold silence when asked about the fortress and the guard. He'd departed with a simple warning, ordering Falken to stay away from everyone else inside the Fortress of Rain.

But now something told him he didn't want to know the reasons why Domlen had entered wearing the long knife with the strange magic aura. Instead of asking, Falken picked up his spoon again and set to work on the soup.

He pushed the bowl away when he'd eaten his fill and rubbed absently at the metal bracer on his left forearm where it chafed his skin. The metal was always warm, and not simply from the heat of his body. He loathed the feel of it, but couldn't help touching it, as if he could somehow pry it off if he only tried enough times.

Domlen walked over to him. Falken leaned away, still intimidated by the man's size, despite himself. But Domlen only took up his bowl and the serving tray and left.

The room was very quiet once the door shut. He listened to Domlen's footfalls descending the stairs. He went to the window and looked out on the rain and the gray, watching as Domlen headed back toward the main keep until the man disappeared from view. Then Falken moved to the bookshelves, scanning the titles again. Nothing that would have information on the blood moon. He bitterly wished he had access to a bigger library. The one back at the palace in Teirlan would be great, the massive library at the Vadolcadium even better. He searched his memory for spells that required a blood moon or whose efficacy could be amplified by the crimson moon's reign. There were too many possibilities, too many unknowns.

He had drifted off to sleep in a chair by the fire with a history of the clans of Unketoh in his lap when Lord Domlen returned. The sound of the rattling lock woke him. He startled from his dream, disoriented, and knocked the book to the floor as he struggled to stand and face his captor. The room was dark. Night had fallen.

Domlen carried bare steel in his hand. It was the knife he'd worn earlier. He wore chain mail beneath his cloak and he carried a lantern in his free hand. He crossed the room without a word. Water dripped from the edge of his blade as he raised it to Falken's throat. His storm-gray eyes were cold and expressionless as a dead man's.

He set the lantern down and then took out a set of iron manacles before thrusting them at Falken. "Put these on."

"I suppose you'll stab me if I don't?"

Domlen didn't answer. His expression didn't change. He only held the knife blade poised at Falken's throat, all the threat that was needed.

Falken lifted his arms and pointed to the metal bracer on his left hand. "You don't need that blade with these damn things clamped around my wrists."

"You tried to kill me with a bust of the god of love. Remember?"

Falken gave him a wry smile. "I'm glad the irony was not wasted on you," he said with more confidence than he actually felt. "So does this mean you'll finally tell me what this is all about? The kidnapping. The ghosts. One man alone in a haunted castle."

"No," was all the other man said. Then he shook the manacles again and the edge of the blade slipped closer, actually touching Falken's skin now.

He didn't move. He could tell the knife was razor-sharp, and it felt oddly warm. If someone had told him a year ago he'd be trapped in a place like this, with a blade at his throat and wielded by a deranged man, he would've laughed himself sick. If only his ruthless and power-hungry brothers could see him now. They would laugh themselves sick as well.

May they choke on their laughter and die, he prayed, then realized it was a poor prayer and likely would not be answered. It didn't matter. None of his prayers had been answered of late.

Slowly, Falken took the manacles and clamped them on his wrists over the metal bracers. The locks clicked as they closed. Domlen tugged on the clasps, ensuring they were locked tight. He pointed toward the door. "Go."

"You don't have to do this," Falken said, holding the man's gaze but hating the pleading quality that had crept into his voice. "My father will pay a huge ransom for my safe return. You could go anywhere. Leave this place. Live somewhere warm, with an actual sun."

"*Go.*"

Falken turned and went. Domlen gathered his lantern and opened the door for him, keeping the blade ready should he try anything. He didn't. He'd learned the hard way that without his magic, he was no threat to the bigger man.

The landing beyond the room was nearly pitch-black until Domlen stepped out with the lantern and drove the darkness off. Falken started toward the stairs leading downward, but Domlen stopped him by raising his arm and barring the way.

"No," Domlen said, pointing. "Up."

Falken looked where the man indicated. There was another set of stairs leading upward onto the roof of the tower. He followed them, his heart beating dully in his chest, his blood rushing in his ears. His thoughts were blurring through his brain, but none of them seemed to be of any use.

He had no magic. No weapons. His hands were bound. He didn't know if the ghosts could harm him, but Domlen certainly could. Domlen pushed past him and shouldered open the trap door at the top of the stairs. It fell open with a bang that echoed throughout the fortress. Then he dragged Falken into the night.

There was no wind, but the rain was a constant drizzle. There were puddles gathered in the uneven spots in the stones. More water ran in little streams along the battlements atop the tower and poured from the sides through holes at the base of the crenels. But his heart sank when he saw what was arranged in the center of the wide tower's battlements. He instantly recognized the paraphernalia for major spell craft. A focus circle had been chiseled into the stone floor with exacting care. It had to have always been here however. He would've heard Domlen doing the work if that weren't the case, and even from this far away, he could see the craftsmanship was exacting. In the center of the circle was a small mixing altar: a metal-banded, clay bowl on a small stand. Braziers stood outside the circle, at right angles, making a square. The coals on the braziers glowed red, protected from the rain by slanted iron caps. They threw their smoldering light across the top of the tower. There was a closed oilskin bag stuffed full of things he couldn't see. Ingredients or power-grevkas and perhaps a book, he guessed. Another small wooden stand sat nearby, but he didn't immediately recognize what it was meant for. It gave off an aura of mystical power too. Domlen walked to the stand and placed the long dagger on its grooves. The moment the blade touched the wood, the metal turned a bright and strange green.

"You're a necromancer after all," Falken said. His voice

was a harsh, ragged sound he barely recognized.

"No."

"A sorcerer then. Don't lie to me. Ghosts did not set this up here." He stared at the meticulous arrangement. It had been done by someone either rigorously precise or highly motivated to be perfect.

"I did it. Now move into the circle."

But Falken discovered that he couldn't obey. His feet wouldn't move. His legs felt as if they were made of straw and at any instant they would give out, sending him reeling like a drunken man.

"Royal blood," Falken whispered. "Royal blood on the blood moon, as Vosk rules the night sky. I'm a fool. I should've seen it."

"I'm sorry," Domlen said.

Falken stared at him, meaning to tell him he could cram his sorry right back down his own throat, but when he met the other man's gaze, he froze with the words unspoken. He could see it in Domlen's eyes. The man truly was sorry. He looked haggard, haunted even. But the fact that he was sorry didn't seem to dissuade him. He still moved to Falken and pushed him gently but irresistibly toward the focus circle.

The rain drizzled down. His boots sloshed in the water as he crossed over the carven border of the focus circle. With the bracers on and denying him access to magic, he could feel nothing when he passed the edge. He looked up at the sky, wondering where that damned blood moon was, if it had reached its apex yet, because he couldn't see it through the dark blanket of clouds. He'd never liked that moon or any of the dark lore and legends surrounding it. The crimson moon had been his eldest brother Tobias's favorite. His brother had called it the murderer's moon.

Yet another item on the list of reasons why he didn't like Tobias either.

Lord Domlen forced him to his knees. He went unwillingly, but the man was too strong. Water soaked through his breeches, feeling cold and unpleasant against his knees and shins.

"Almost time now," Domlen said softly. He began to add ingredients and powders to the clay and metal altar. Gem dust. Crystals. Bone fragments. Rare plant leaves. An ebony grevka carved into the shape of Vosk. He wasn't consulting a book, perhaps because of the rain, but if the complex spell worked and he'd prepared it all from memory, then Falken would be truly impressed.

He would be very dead...but impressed.

A cough of pained laughter burst from his lips. Domlen glanced at him, frowning, no doubt wondering what in the world the crazed prince still had to laugh about. He didn't know either. Being dead didn't seem amusing now that it seemed like an onrushing inevitability. Being bound in the rain, helpless, hungry, no magic, no hope, moments from having his royal blood used as the critical ingredient to power a spell made dealing with court intrigues seem like a ride through a summer meadow on a magical horse made of diamonds.

As Falken watched the man work, part of his mind desperately tried to convince him that this was nothing but a dream. He was safe in bed. Domlen would soon shake him awake for his foul breakfast. Falken would try again to seduce him or perhaps try and hit him with something heavy. Domlen would glower and brood and take away his makeshift weapons as if he were a small child...

This was all a bad dream.

Except it wasn't.

Domlen's hands were skilled. His measurements were precise and careful, spilling nothing. As soon as Domlen finished filling the altar, Falken lurched to his feet. His knees almost gave out. He staggered before drawing back his boot to kick over the altar and spill all the precious ingredients. He could imagine the beautiful look on Domlen's face when he watched all his careful preparation end up in the puddles.

Domlen was quicker. He stepped in front of Falken and hurled him to the ground before he could aim his kick. Falken hit the stone hard, a grunt escaping his lips as the breath was knocked from him.

"You're a brave man," Lord Domlen said. "I know you want to live. But this is bigger than either of us. Know that you will die a hero."

"Hero? I'll simply be dead. Murdered. By you."

Domlen scowled at him, but he did not say different. Instead, he snarled, "On your knees in the circle. Face away from me. Don't move again or I will truss you like a pig."

The crazed urge to run at the battlements and throw himself from the tower seized him. But as soon as it flashed into his mind, the strength to actually attempt it left him. He almost attempted it anyway, and damn his captor and damn his spells to the darkest pit. Then again, what did it matter? He would be dead either way.

Facing away from Domlen now, he could no longer watch the man finish his preparations. He was breathing in desperate little gasps, feeling himself tremble, hating the fear that had him in its grip. He didn't want to die. Gods above, he did not want to die.

The air around them began to shimmer with a green-blue fire. It was nearly intangible, like glowing cobwebs. Domlen had set the spell in motion, initiating the reactions. If not for these cursed bracers, Falken would've been able to feel the incredible power of the magic gathering inside the circle, ready to be used.

He heard the rattle of metal on wood as Domlen picked up the dagger from the stand, apparently finished with his preparations. The sound went through him like an arrow.

"Speak your last request," Domlen said from behind him. His voice sounded strained, though Falken couldn't tell if that was from the force of the magic around them or because he was about to kill another man. Yet Falken could *feel* the dagger hovering above him, ready to open him up.

A last request? He laughed again—the sound a mix of half-choked sob and a guffaw. "I have a thousand last requests. I'll tell you all of them and you can help me pick." That way they'd be here all night, and Falken could continue living for a little while longer.

But Domlen only said, "Pick one."

"I want to see the sun again."

There was an excruciatingly long silence from behind him. He waited, breathing fast, the rain running down his face like tears.

"I do too," Domlen finally answered. Then he set his hand on Falken's head and bunched his fist in his hair. Almost gently, he drew Falken's head back to expose his throat. The green blade was glowing, throwing wavering light across the stonework.

Falken watched the knife move closer to his throat. He couldn't help the moan of fear that escaped him. He hated himself for making that sound, although he believed the gods would understand.

"I'm sorry," Domlen told him, and there seemed to be so

much regret packed into the words that for a moment Falken believed him completely. Believed him completely…and hated him for doing this with all his heart.

As the man had drawn his head back to fully expose his neck, he was left staring up into Domlen's eyes. He brought the glowing knife closer to Falken's throat. Heat seemed to pour off the blade. Falken twisted, trying to stay as far from it as possible. He was shaking so badly that his teeth were rattling.

Then Lord Domlen shoved him forward with an anguished cry. Falken barely managed to twist and hit the wet, cold stone of the tower with his shoulder. He lay there panting, still shaking. Slowly he turned to look at the man who wanted to kill him.

Domlen stared at the knife in his hand. His face held an expression of abject horror and a loss so keen it touched Falken's heart, even after all that had happened. Even after the blade had been an instant from killing him. The other man met and held Falken's stare. Everything seemed to slow, to narrow down to the both of them, in the dark, in the rain, with the knife.

Then Domlen turned on his heel and walked out of the focus circle.

But as his captor left the circle, the unused power of the spell rebounded on him, sending him staggering before smashing him to his knees. Domlen screamed in agony. The dagger clattered along the stones, throwing its eerie green light.

Some ferocious-animal part of Falken wanted to crawl his way over to the dagger, grab it, and stab Domlen. Hadn't he already tried to kill the man once? And that had been before Domlen tried to use his lifeblood to power a blood moon

spell. But he didn't move. He only lay curled up inside the
focus circle, pressed to the cold stones and weak as a kitten,
watching as Domlen ever so slowly pushed himself back to
his feet. The man looked deathly pale, his limbs were shaking,
and his steps were more staggering lurches than anything
else.

He didn't look back as he collected the dagger and made
his way to the trapdoor leading from the top of the tower. He
descended slowly, like a man who'd seen a hundred or more
years in his life, and disappeared from sight.

Eventually, Falken forced himself to get back to his feet
and leave the circle. He was not hit with a reflexive backlash
of magic. All that power had struck at Domlen alone. The
ingredients for the spell inside the altar were all burned away,
charred, used up. His manacles clinked as he stumbled his
way to the trap door. There was no sign of Domlen anywhere.
Could he have gone? Or died? The raw power from the spell
rebounding onto him when he'd left the focus circle without
successfully finishing the magic easily could have killed him.
He was lucky to have been able to walk away at all.

But Falken was no longer imprisoned inside his tower
room. He looked at the dark stairs descending the tower, then
he took the lantern Domlen had left behind when he'd
stumbled away. His heart was pounding hard and fast as he
made his way down the stairs, clutching at the wall to keep
from falling. He was so full of hope and the yearning for
freedom that he wouldn't even allow himself to think lest he
curse his chances. Thinking might mean this was all some
nightmare and he would awake still a captive—an ironic turn
from the very thing he'd wished for only moments ago.

He finally made it to the bottom of the tower stairs. The
heavy double doors were shut. He scrambled to them and

threw his weight against them. They did not move. He pawed at the handles, but they refused to turn. Locked. Domlen had locked them and taken the key, the bastard. Falken was hoping the injured man had made a mistake and forgotten.

He sagged against the doors. He could *feel* his freedom just on the other side of the doors, so very close. But instead, he was trapped in here, bound by manacles, the crovmane bracers still cutting him off from his magic. He was still imprisoned, wondering if Domlen had gone off to die somewhere in the castle and whether he'd be left to starve to death in the tower. Wondering why Domlen had spared him. Wondering if he'd truly been spared at all.

He wept then. All the things he'd endured since his capture rebounded upon him with the force of a thwarted spell. He sagged against the locked doors and he wept.

* * *

Domlen finally staggered into his quarters, grunting with pain, clutching his sides as white-hot agony pierced him with every step. Blood seeped from his mouth and spattered in droplets from his nose like red rain. He used the walls for support as he made his way toward his bedroom, gasping in air in big gulps. His ignorance of magic had cost him dearly. He was a fool, toying with something he did not understand, and now he would pay the price.

He thought he might be dying. The possibility didn't bring him fear. He was in too much pain to feel any fear.

He almost made it to his bedroom. His strength gave out in front of the hearth, and he collapsed to the cold stone. He couldn't find the resolve to push himself back to his feet. Instead, he decided to stay there, wet and shivering in the draft from the empty fireplace. There were few things sadder than a cold hearth, he realized, as a fresh convulsion of pain wracked him.

The pain had struck him the instant he'd stepped outside the focus circle. Even a novice could guess what had happened. All his work and careful planning had been undone when he'd started the spell but hadn't spilled the royal blood it required. He'd been meticulous in his preparation for the curse-breaking ritual. He'd laid the groundwork for it, meticulously collecting the required ingredients and items, months before making the journey to Teirlan and capturing Falken. He'd used the detailed drawings and designs given to him by a warlock called Vendle in the southern marshes. In payment for the counter-spell, he'd given his gold and his blood, then endured the spiritual trial Vendle had set him on that had nearly broken his mind and left him drained and empty in the swamp. He'd even acquired a plague dagger — the ceremonial knife with the green blade that amplified blood magic, said to have been forged by early sects worshipping Vosk, the crimson moon. Thinking back, he shouldn't have been surprised when the gathered energy rebounded on him after he failed to complete the ritual and give purpose to the power. But he was no sorcerer. He only knew, with exacting detail, what he was supposed to do to break the curse. Unintended effects were not his foray.

Now all that effort and suffering and preparation was lost because the man he'd needed to kill had wanted to see the sun again. No, that was part of it, but not all. It had been Falken's eyes. The moment when Domlen had stared down into those eyes and realized how afraid the man was, saw the panic in his soul as he realized how badly he wanted to live. He'd held the blade in his hand, seeing the wavering image of its green metal as it shimmered of its own accord, and he'd known that he was the monster here. That moment, he'd realized he couldn't kill an innocent man, no matter how badly his people needed to be set free. No matter how great the threat from the revenir.

He simply could not do it.

He considered making another try to reach his bedroom, but the strength wasn't in him. He didn't even have the strength to kick off his wet boots or shrug out of his soaked clothing. A groan slipped from his lips. His muscles felt as if he'd overstrained them while working too hard at swordplay. He sighed out a shuddering breath.

Even breathing hurt.

Falken. His thoughts always turned back to the prince. He wouldn't kill him. He couldn't. Yet, he suspected it went even deeper than respect for the life of another human being. He always found himself looking forward to the times during the day when he'd be able to see the man. Even if it involved something as tedious as delivering Falken's meals and switching out his chamber pot and removing the dirty bedding and clothes to be washed. Before the curse, such work would've been beneath him. Now he not only didn't mind the menial chores, he actively looked forward to it. Surprising, yet it was a break from the sameness that weighed so heavily upon him. Before Falken, every day was identical to the last. The ghosts did not change. The weather did not change. The food did not change. Besides, the chores allowed him to be around the prince. Even if they did not say a single word to one another, it gave him a chance to see the other man. He'd been leery of that urge, and rightfully so. Because in the end it had ruined him and everything he'd planned.

He carefully rolled himself over onto his back, staring up at the stone arches that supported the ceiling. Perhaps he should crawl his way to Yosel. The old scholar was no sorcerer either, but he knew healing with herbs and medicines. He might know more about what had happened to Domlen when he'd left the focus circle. Perhaps the old man could tell him whether or not he would die...

And death might even have been tempting, except that it meant giving up on his people. But hadn't he already done that? If he couldn't bring himself to kill Falken, then the people he loved and cared for were doomed. He had failed them all.

As for his death, he'd know the outcome soon enough. If he survived the night, he was likely to survive the day. He would trudge on, hour by hour if he had to. If he lived, he had no idea what he would say to Falken when he saw him again. The prince was a sorcerer from the royal line, a mystic sage from Vadolcadium. He would've guessed what the ritual was, and there was no mistaking the fact he was intended to be the sacrifice necessary to power it.

The agony squeezed him tighter, until his mind was hazy with pain. His thoughts tried to flee the suffering, escaping into old memories. They drifted back to the trials in the swamp, when he'd taken the foul potion Vendle had given him only a moment before shoving him into the black water. He'd floated in the currents like a corpse, plagued by visions, by memories of the Boa Visk attacking his home. Images came into his mind of his hand wielding his sword, fighting at the breach in the wall, killing Boa Visk on the fateful day they'd blocked out the sun and weakened the spells inside the stone.

Memories of one of the deadly, snake-like creatures pinning him down, grinning its yellowed fangs while its amber slit-eyes flashed. It tried to tear out his throat, but he'd stabbed it with a dagger before it could. Images from after the fall of the fortress—glimpses of Prince Falken stalking through the forest, believing he was hunting a drake, right before Domlen sprang his trap, incapacitating him and binding him with the bracers. The bracers were another "gift" from the warlock. For that gift, he'd paid not with blood or with gold but with his essence, a shard of his own life force. Vendle had stolen three years off the end of his life. But why would Domlen care about that cost? Once he freed his people from their horrible fate, there was nothing left for him. There was no more Fortress of the Sun. Let the haunted, derelict place it had become drown in rain and moss. Let it ever be a place even the Boa Visk were afraid to tread.

Domlen curled onto his side, trying to find a position where the pain hurt him least. The potion and the trial had been intended to prove his worth to the warlock...and reveal whether or not he was ready to do what needed to be done. He'd believed he was ready. He had been wrong.

He was weak. He'd believed himself a warrior. A lord defender of the northern passes of the Koltero Mountains. He'd battled the Boa Visk, enduring their siege for months, costing them thousands of lives. Even if they'd been victorious in the end, even if they had broken the stronghold open with the counter magic guilty of spawning the curse, they were gone and he was not.

Despite all that, when the hour had finally come, he had proven himself unable to do what was necessary, unable to kill another man. He'd let his loneliness and his desire and his weak need for love unman him when he'd needed to be strongest, when his will should have been steel. He deserved to die...and couldn't, because he still had to find some way to keep the poor souls trapped in this fortress from turning into revenir bent on ravaging the living.

Only now he doubted he still had the strength of spirit to do so. Perhaps he'd never had it. He could not find the strength to sacrifice one life for the greater good, for his innocent people, for all the inhabitants of the surrounding lands the revenir would destroy. Because for one thing above all else, Vendle had been quite clear. The Boa Visk magic that had brought the storms had reacted unexpectedly with the spells crafted into the walls. Once the Boa Visk began slaughtering the people inside the fortress, all had been set in motion, and the final result would be desolation for everyone.

Now, if he survived he would face impossible choices. He'd failed. Though he didn't have the steel in him to sacrifice the man he'd kidnapped, the revenir still had to be stopped. His people still had to be set free. Somehow.

Despite his pain and exhaustion, sleep was a long time coming. The pain haunted him into his dreams.

CHAPTER FIVE

The sound of the key rattling in the lock woke Falken from more nightmares the next morning. He rolled out of bed with a groan and quickly pulled on his breeches. He was done with parading around naked, attempting to draw the other man into a physical relationship. He supposed that after nearly being ritually sacrificed on the night of a blood moon, his cock no longer felt perky about the challenge of seduction.

He had no idea what would happen now. He'd resigned himself to that. Last night he'd come closer to death than ever before. He had also come closer to escaping than ever before. Now here he was, still a captive, yet still drawing air and grateful for it. Long ago he'd believed death would be preferable to losing his magic. He could now say with confidence he had been entirely wrong.

When the door creaked all the way open, he was stunned

by what he saw. Lord Domlen's clothing was the same from last night, wrinkled and still damp. His face was haggard and drawn, with lines that hadn't been there a day ago. The man had always moved with power and a predator grace warriors often possessed, but now he entered the room like an old man whose joints pained him. As Domlen came closer carrying the tray with his meal, Falken noticed dark spatters of blood on the man's tunic and breeches and more dotting the tips of his boots.

And yet, Domlen was still alive—still, in fact, dutifully bringing him breakfast. Although the damage caused by prematurely breaking the spell had been inflicted upon both his body and his spirit-soul, it said much about the man's incredible strength and willpower that he hadn't died on the spot.

Lord Domlen noticed his scrutiny. His lips twitched into a tight-lipped smile, which came as another surprise.

"Your meal," he said, his voice raspy and barely above a whisper.

Falken watched him with a mix of reluctant admiration and dread as Domlen shambled to the table and set the tray down. Once there however, he paused and closed his eyes, gripping the edge of the table as if for balance. Sweat ran down his forehead. His broad shoulders were hunched.

"It's cold today," Domlen said, starting toward the hearth. "Need a fire..."

Falken moved toward the table, plagued by conflicting thoughts. Domlen was clearly hurt. Now would be the perfect time to kill him, take the keys, and escape when the man was weak. This was the moment he'd waited for. Last night Domlen meant to sacrifice him. Falken should rightfully be dead. He'd been completely in the other man's power. If

Domlen hadn't stayed his hand at the last moment—

At the hearth, Domlen suddenly stumbled and collapsed. He hit the stone around the hearth with a grunt. He sprawled there, his breathing rasping and shallow, one of his large hands twitching feebly.

"Always falling in front of a cold fireplace..." he said in a weak voice, and at first Falken thought he was coughing, until he realized the sound was Domlen's laughter. That laughter simultaneously sent chills down his spine and sparked pity in his heart.

Falken's blood was rushing through his veins and roaring in his ears. He couldn't move. He only stood there, staring at the fallen man. Part of him feared this was some kind of trick. Some kind of test. The rest of him wanted to hurry to his aid. The sight of the man he'd believed he hated lying on the ground, breathing hard, shaking feebly and wracked with pain should've made him feel triumphant, but it didn't. Not in the least.

He made no conscious decision. He simply hurried to Domlen's side and knelt down. Domlen's eyes had fluttered closed. He put a hand on the man's shoulder and shook him, calling his name. It took more strength to move him than he'd expected. His captor was heavy, and his shoulder was thick with muscle, but his skin also blazed with heat.

Domlen's eyes blinked open, but he was staring off into the distance, seeming unaware of his surroundings. "The blood moon..." he whispered as a rivulet of red trickled from the corner of his mouth. "The blood moon..."

"What about the blood moon?" Falken asked, leaning closer. This was not good at all. The stubborn fool should've been in his own bed, clinging to life. Instead, he'd gone to prepare Falken's meal and then climbed all those stairs. The man was insane.

"It returns…soon…" Domlen whispered, so softly that Falken barely caught the words.

Heart pounding hard, Falken settled back on his boot heels, watching as his captor's eyes closed again. The blood moon returns soon. He had no almanac in this tower room, but the paths and appearances of the multiple moons across the sky could be complex. But if Domlen said soon, it conditions could repeat this far north in as little as eight days.

Why else would Domlen whisper about the blood moon unless he meant to attempt the ritual again?

He reached out and took one of the pieces of chopped wood stacked near the hearth. It was awkward to hold, but he could manage to use it as a club, gripping it in two hands. He could crush Domlen's skull. He could end this now. The man could do nothing to stop him. He was utterly helpless. Now was the time to set himself free.

Instead, he set the log down again. Domlen did not stir. His breathing was erratic. His pulse felt weak and thready. His skin felt feverishly hot.

He was dying.

The keys were in the pocket of Domlen's tunic. Falken reached out, breathing fast, and slipped his hand inside. The cold key ring brushed his fingers. He grabbed it and pulled it free. The keys jangled. The sound was beautiful to his ears.

The walk to the door of his tower room was one of the longest of his life. With every step, he anticipated Domlen waking up and coming after him. The man was going to try and kill him again on the next blood moon. And Falken was a fool not to finish him off when he had the chance. He glanced over his shoulder again, hesitating and undecided, feeling sick to his stomach.

The man was dying. Falken didn't have to do a thing, only walk away, find the gap in the fortress wall, and start his journey home.

But what if Domlen didn't die? What if the man came after him again? The next time, Falken might not be so lucky. Unless...

The bracers cutting him off from his magic were still locked around his wrists. A thrill shot through him and his heart soared as he fumbled through the keys. He tried the smaller ones on the mechanisms where the clamps locked together on the underside of the bracers. He stopped breathing entirely when he found one, worked it inside, and heard the click of the lock springing open.

The bracer tumbled to the floor with a *clunk*. His pulse beat in his ears as he shifted the key ring to his other hand and unlocked the other bracer. It also fell, hit the stone, and went spinning off. He snatched up each of the hated things, holding them as if they were live serpents, and flung them out the open tower window. He didn't hear them strike the ground.

A shudder of pure delight went through him at the incredible feeling of freedom. It was as if a black curtain had been between him and the light of his power and now that curtain was ripped away. He couldn't match Domlen's raw strength, but now that he had his magic back, he didn't need to. He could kill the other man with a spell from across the room.

But he'd never used his magic to kill another human being. Monsters, yes, when they threatened the people of Teirlan. This would be cold-blooded murder. It was strange, because he had already attacked Domlen once with that intention, and seconds ago he had considered killing his captor with a piece of firewood...and yet something about using magic to kill a helpless man, enemy or not, seemed particularly foul to him.

But Domlen had meant to murder him.

Yet, he hadn't. At the last moment, he hadn't.

So why had he been whispering about the blood moon again?

He finally tore his gaze away from Domlen, still sprawled unmoving in front of the cold hearth. He couldn't do it. Yes, he'd been ready to slay the man from an ambush, but now that Domlen was helpless, he simply couldn't find it inside his heart to take his life. Before, he'd been desperate, but now he was free.

Instead, he went to the door. He knew the exact key for it. He'd watched Domlen use it often enough. His hand was trembling as he slipped the key into the lock and turned. Relief washed through him when the lock disengaged and he pulled the door open. He let out a long, shuddering breath at regaining his freedom after all this time and all that had happened.

Behind him, Domlen groaned. Falken spun toward him, but the other man still wasn't awake. Falken felt another surge of pity for him before he squashed the emotion. He stepped through the doorway onto the landing and then paused again. Should he lock Domlen inside? It would serve him right, and it would ensure that the other man did not chase him. Although it would likely mean Domlen would starve to death inside. There were only ghosts here, and he wasn't sure how much the spirits trapped in the fortress could manipulate the things around them. Most phantoms could, to varying degrees, but did he want to leave a man to slowly starve? Did he want that on his conscience? If he intended to kill Domlen, he should do it clean and painlessly.

Besides, he had his magic back. He didn't need to lock the man away in the tower. He would not be surprised again, and if Domlen pursued him, he would discover just what a Vadolcadium-trained sorcerer of the royal line of Teirlan was capable of.

He took his first step outside the room as a free man.

And stopped.

He should be running for the fortress walls, searching for the way out, but his legs wouldn't obey. All he knew was that this didn't feel right. It felt like something his brothers would do—leave a man to die without a backward glance or a second thought.

He was clearly a madman. He shouldn't do this. And yet here he was, walking back inside the room he loathed, heading toward the man who kidnapped him, kept him imprisoned, and had meant to kill him. He knelt down beside Domlen and felt his pulse again. Still weak and erratic. He was no talented healer, but all sorcerers learned some basic curative magic. Whether or not he succeeded, trying to heal Domlen would weaken him considerably, for a time at least. These weren't magics that came easily to him. Any attempt would be akin to shoving a boulder up a hill.

He laughed, and the sound of his laughter echoing back to him sounded quite mad. That made him laugh harder. He had no idea why he found any of this funny, save that he couldn't believe he had not only stopped himself from leaving, but he was going to use his strength to heal his enemy.

He gently grabbed Domlen under the shoulders and grunted as he dragged the man toward the tower room's bed. Speaking of shoving boulders up a hill, by the gods was the man heavy. It took more effort than he expected to pull his limp weight across the room. Then he nearly broke his back hauling Domlen from the floor onto the bed.

Domlen groaned and his eyes fluttered. "Wanted the sun..." he whispered, followed by a lot of words Falken couldn't make out.

"Don't we all," Falken murmured. But Domlen had faded out of consciousness again. His skin was blazing hot, but he was shivering. The trickle of blood from his mouth had started again.

He straightened Domlen on the bed so he was lying on his back. Then he unlaced the man's tunic and bared his chest. Dark hair spread on his broad upper chest and another patch gathered around his navel and traveled farther downward, disappearing below his belt. There was a large, jagged scar on his chest as well, cutting downward from his nipple to his below his navel. An old war wound?

Falken shook his head and forced himself to focus. He placed his hands over Domlen's heart. This was the life force core of the man. His center. This would help move the magic through his body.

Using magic after so long was difficult and painfully slow. It didn't help that he was attempting to heal, and healing had never been his forte. Beneath his hands, Domlen's heartbeat at first grew more erratic and his skin even hotter. Falken used the connection between them, the touch of skin against skin, to seek out the harm done to him and then to channel his power to heal it. He was soon sweating freely. His healing was clumsy and draining, but as the minutes passed, Domlen's heartbeat steadied and his breathing grew less labored. At last, utterly drained, he drew away and sagged into one of the chairs.

He had done all he could do. He didn't know if it would be enough, but he was too weak to keep at it. Using magic was like using a muscle...and because of those damned crovmane bracers, he was long out of practice.

Domlen seemed to have slipped into a more restful state. He no longer felt as hot, and the trickle of blood had stopped. The damage Falken had first sensed inside him when he'd begun healing had been staggering. It was amazing Domlen had been able to get out of bed at all this morning. A normal man probably would've died last night after leaving the focus circle with the spell incomplete.

He brought one of the thin blankets up and tucked it around Domlen. Next, he took one of the cloths near the water basin, wet it, and used it to clean the man's face and wipe away his sweat. That done, he simply sat on the edge of the bed beside Domlen, staring at the man's haggard face. He should be running southward for the valley right now. He should be planning what he would tell his father to explain his long absence. Once he'd even dreamed of leading an army here to exact vengeance on the man who had imprisoned him.

Instead, he sat next to the man and gently touched his hand. He had no idea what would happen now. That scared him and it thrilled him at the same time. Gently, he brushed a lock of Domlen's dark hair away from his pale face.

He wondered if Domlen would die, despite all his efforts.

He wondered why he cared.

* * *

There were dreams, nightmarish, feverish and frantic, but

they vanished from Domlen's mind the instant he clawed his way back to wakefulness.

His head was spinning. Part of the reason for the spinning was because something or someone was shaking him. He cracked open an eye. A blurry image of Falken's face appeared before him. He flinched and blinked rapidly, trying to clear his vision. His heart lurched in his chest. He expected to see a weapon in Falken's hands, right before the man killed him with it. But Falken's hands were empty—completely bare. The bracers were gone...

He tried to sit up. It took all his strength just to rise halfway, and Falken set a hand on his chest and gently pushed him back down. He was far too weak to resist.

"Be easy," Falken said. "You're badly hurt."

Domlen opened his mouth to reply, but only a croak escaped. Falken reached behind him and poured water from the pitcher into a cup. Then he brought the cup to Domlen's lips, tilting his head to help him drink.

His thoughts were all confused, fuzzy. He wasn't even sure if this was real or another feverish dream.

"Why am I alive?" he finally managed to ask. His voice sounded rough and torn. Barely recognizable.

"You may yet die."

Domlen looked into the other man's eyes. He tried to decipher whether Falken was referring to the harm Domlen had suffered when he'd broken the spell casting or whether Falken meant he might still kill Domlen himself. He couldn't tell, but he thought it an even chance either way.

When Domlen didn't respond, Falken stood and walked away. It took a lot of effort to turn his head to watch the other man, but he managed it. He wanted to ask him to come back and stay with him for a moment but feared Falken would refuse. He needn't have worried. A moment later, Falken returned carrying the bowl of mutton, pickled greens, and soaked grain mix Domlen had brought him earlier... Was it only this morning? He had only vague memories of making the meal and crossing the fortress to bring in here. It all seemed hazy. Dreamlike.

"Now *you* get to suffer through this slop you love to feed me," Falken said with a grin. "I must admit, I'm looking forward to this."

Domlen smiled. "I eat the same food as you do."

Falken was looking at him strangely.

"What is it?" he asked, wondering if he'd started bleeding from the mouth again.

"That is the first genuine smile I've ever seen on your face. You almost look like a human being when you smile."

That earned a scowl. "What do I usually look like?"

"A gargoyle struggling to move his bowels. In the rain."

He couldn't help it, he laughed. It was weak. It hurt. It immediately turned into coughs. But the sound brought a warm smile to Falken's face. He realized that was the first true smile he'd ever seen on the other man as well. It lit up his eyes, made him seem alive, vivacious. He had to look away first, aware that he was staring.

Falken held the bowl in front of him while he worked the spoon. His hands shook so badly he spilled at least half of every spoonful. Falken never protested or took over, never sighed with impatience. And he did not leave either.

When his stomach was full enough, he nudged at the bowl with the back of his hand and Falken took it away.

"It is measly fare," Domlen admitted, oddly enough feeling sensitive about the fact that he had nothing better to feed the other man. "But it is all that's left in the fortress.

Casks of salted mutton. Pickled greens. A little grain that the rats haven't been into yet." He hesitated, and then pressed on. "There is enough left for perhaps two more months and then there will be nothing."

Falken moved to the hearth and added a few logs to the fire he'd built, then came back to the bed and sat on the edge once more. They stared at each other. It was very quiet, and all that could be heard was the constant patter of raindrops outside. Then Falken reached into his tunic and withdrew the black iron ring with its collection of keys. He held it up, and the keys made a metallic clatter. His gaze was challenging, defiant. Domlen could hardly blame him.

He took a deep breath, which hurt inside his chest and he coughed. He wiped at his mouth and his hand came away bloody. They both looked at the blood, but neither of them said a word about it.

Instead, he said, "You have the keys...and you didn't leave. Why?" He could not wrap his thoughts around it. He had ambushed and subdued the man, kidnapped him, dragged him hundreds of leagues from his homeland.

Locked him in a tower.

Had nearly taken his life.

And yet, here Falken was. Not only had he not killed Domlen when he'd been most vulnerable, he'd hauled him onto the bed. Tended him. Helped him eat.

"Why?" Falken repeated, tilting his head and seeming to consider the question. "I should have killed you. I was tempted. Either finish you or leave you locked in this damned room. Poetic justice." He shook his head. "But I am not that kind of person. So I tried to heal you with what crude curative magics I know. It may not have been enough, but I've done what I can."

He had no reply to that. The simple statement was humbling. He likely owed his life to this man.

Falken turned to stare at the fire. In the gray, rainy gloom the heat and light was a blessing. "Then again, you didn't kill me last night during the blood moon. In truth, not killing me might have killed you." He clenched his fist around the keys. "So before I leave, I want to know every bit of the truth. And you owe it to me. But start with why you brought me here."

Did he owe Prince Falken the truth? Yes, the man had more than earned it.

"I needed the blood of a royal line to break the curse," he said. "The night of a pure blood moon, sacrificing one of royal birth would power my counter-spell. You guessed as much during the ritual."

Falken held up a hand for him to slow down. "You're no sorcerer. The magic you set in motion was powerful and dangerous. How did you learn to cast a spell that complex?" But before Domlen could answer, Falken was already shaking his head. "No, I'm getting ahead of myself. There's so much I don't know. Start at the beginning."

So he took a moment to collect his thoughts. He was already exhausted. The sudden changes between the two of them had left him reeling. For such a long time, he'd struggled to hide the truth from Falken, but now so much had changed that trying to hide it would be foolish and vain. He looked Falken in the eyes and began to tell the tale.

* * *

"Six years ago, the Boa Visk sent an army through the

Koltero Mountains," Lord Domlen said. "They came up the Crydale Pass. The Fortress of the Sun was built to defend that pass against invaders. That was my charge."

Although Domlen tried to keep his voice neutral and the emotion suppressed, Falken could still sense the pain of his memories like earth tremors below the surface of his words. He expected this would be hard on the man. A story that ended in the need for blood could not be a happy one. Yet, even if it hurt him to relive it, Falken still deserved to know the truth.

Domlen continued. "I am lord of the fortress, appointed by King Leovic of Tharsgald, and I led the defense. At first, the Boa Visk gave us an ultimatum. Open our gates or everyone inside the walls would be slaughtered. Before the enemy engaged us, I sent off riders to request aid from my king and any and all who could come to our relief. Then I refused the enemy's terms. The fortress only exists to guard the valleys and lands from these mountains to the sea. It was my duty to hold at all costs."

Prince Falken had never been in a large-scale war. Teirlan had been sheltered from attack from the Boa Visk by the Bitter Sea and a vast desert, except for a small border shared with Tyrdenva. All across that border there had been battle with the Boa Visk, who had once seemed unstoppable, but those battles had taken place when Falken had not been old enough to fight. But in Tyrdenva and other lands, there had been tales of human armies regrouping under powerful generals like Hormask and Cyrdath and reclaiming the lands they'd lost. The Boa Visk had ceased attacking Teirlan to try and hold what they'd already conquered. Since then, Teirlan had experience relative peace.

"How long until you could expect relief from the attack?"

he asked gently.

"Months. But this is a strong place." Domlen's voice shone with pride. "An ancient place. Spells were built into the stonework making the fortifications nearly unbreakable. The wall towers have commanding defensive positions, and because of the steep slopes coming out of the pass, it is difficult to deploy an army and siege engines against us."

"And did your king send relief?"

"No reinforcements came. At first I feared my riders were all slain or the king had no help to send because Tharsgald was hard beset from all sides. It was years later, on my journey southward seeking a way to break the curse, that I learned the king had been slain by Boa Visk assassins and the lords and lands of Tharsgald were in utter chaos."

Falken nodded slowly. He did know that Tharsgald's king had been murdered and his son had been too young to rule effectively. The lands had become unstable, seeing the rise of individual lords commanding strong local power and fortified city-states. In such chaos, it was little wonder no relief had come.

"The men and women who live here are strong, brave people," Domlen said. "It was an honor to lead them. We threw back every attack they sent against us. We held for six months. We made the Boa Visk bleed. We threw down their ladders. We smashed their rams. Their spells could not bring our warded battlements down." He shook his head and closed his eyes. He slowly leaned his head back, his mouth thinning into a tight line. "But the Boa Visk sorcerers discovered the flaw in our defenses. The ancient spells that protected the walls drew their power from solartia."

It suddenly made more sense why this place had been named the Fortress of the Sun—for solartia, not simply for a tower that reflected sunbeams. If the spells the builders had woven into the fortifications relied upon sunlight for power, as many of the ancient magics did, then they would weaken if long periods of darkness followed. He was passing familiar with the raw mystical energy of solartia and its use, although it was not his bailiwick. The spells would be charged by sunlight. The power it drew was unending, but using solartia was risky. The spells would wane and weaken overnight before waxing in strength again as the dawn broke. But Lord Domlen had often referred to this place the Fortress of Rain…

"They started a storm, didn't they?" Falken asked quietly. "To nullify the defenses. To cut off the power activating the spells."

Domlen nodded, coughed, and wiped away another smear of blood. The blood disturbed Falken most. It spoke of harm done deep inside the other man's body that his crude attempt at healing had not completely fixed.

"The Boa Visk sorcerers created a storm that raged with rain and lightning and covered the sky for leagues. The storm lasted for twenty-three days while we still defended the wall, and then their army attacked again with everything they had. We threw them back from the walls three times. But just past midnight, they finally breached the eastern fortifications. The spells had been weakened too much. We could not hold. The fortress was theirs long before the dawn. Most of my defenders were dead. I was fighting at the breach, but was wounded."

Domlen pulled open his tunic with a trembling hand to reveal the scar slashing downward across his chest, making an ugly trail from his nipple to the patch of dark hair around his navel. The scar tissue had healed badly, leaving a wide, pale mark behind. Falken's hand rose of its own accord and touched the old wound. It was astonishing that the man had survived a wound this severe. Many men would've died from a lesser cut. Domlen was clearly a survivor.

Domlen pulled his tunic down again, brushing aside Falken's touch, but gently. "The Boa Visk were true to their word. They slaughtered my people and kept me alive to watch." He closed his eyes, but not before Falken saw the tears in them. Despite all that had happened, his heart went out to the other man. He couldn't imagine what he'd been through. Domlen's voice, when he spoke again, was so soft it was nearly a whisper. "I watched them all die as it rained. But something went wrong with the spell the Boa Visk used to create the storm. The blood moon was full. The magic unstable. I do not know. But all the death and the mass release of spirits were somehow interfered with by the magic powering the storm. My people rose again as ghosts. Phantoms with no memory of their own deaths."

"What did the Boa Visk do when they lost control of their magic?"

"At first, nothing. They intended to kill me last, but their sorcerers held off on my execution on the chance I was a powerful warlock and had something to do with the ghosts. By then they realized the storm they'd set in motion could no longer be stopped. The ghosts began attacking the Boa Visk, believing they were still defending the fortress. It was chaos. Within three nights, their remaining army had moved on, more retreat than advance. They left no garrison behind. They abandoned the fortress to the ghosts and the rain."

Falken leaned back, riveted by the story, trying to fit all the pieces together. "But they didn't kill you."

"I was the last person alive. They left me in the dungeon to starve. Or perhaps they forgot me. Perhaps they considered me a dead man already and could not be bothered to take the time to make it final." He shook his head. "As I said, everything was chaos—floods, rage storms, hostile ghosts."

"How did you escape the cell?"

"The ghosts can manipulate physical objects. I think they draw power from the storm or the blood moon and it makes them stronger. They do not easily fade. They retain their personalities but cannot form new memories and keep them for long. So Tommick, the captain of the guard, released me from the cell. It was as simple as that. The trapped spirits of all these people I knew were now looking to me to lead, as I always had. I again took up my role as lord of the fortress and began to search for a way to end this curse."

"Magic," Falken prompted with a grim smile. "You tried to study powerful, complex forces as a novice. I admire your confidence, but that is a staggering undertaking for a man without the raw talent. Why didn't you send for help? There are powerful sorcerers in Tharsgald."

"No one came. My people were bound here as ghosts and could not leave the borders of the fortress. The rains flooded the surrounding lands, turning them into swamps, changing creeks into rivers, driving off the few farmers and villagers who hadn't already fled the Boa Visk advance. This unnatural storm ends beyond the valley. It's as if the cloud cover hits a wall and stops. Meanwhile, I struggled to understand what had happened. Many of the tomes in our library are ancient, here from when the fortress was first raised long ago—"

"Those would likely be in High Urrian," Falken broke in. "Can you read the language?"

"No. And I found no answers in the books I could understand. I finally set out alone, headed southward, deeper into Tharsgald to find aid. I was gone for more than a year. I learned much, and none of it good."

Falken had no words to give. He couldn't imagine what it would've been like to be the only survivor of a Boa Visk massacre. Following the trail behind a Boa Visk army rampaging through the lands you'd sworn to protect would've crushed many a man's heart.

"It was a joy to finally leave the storm and the rain behind and feel the sunlight again," Domlen said. "But that was the only joy I ever found. Tharsgald was in turmoil after the king was assassinated. The invading Boa Visk army had been destroyed, but it had cost the lives of many warriors and most of the royal guard. The countryside became the territory of bandits and thieves and small lords using their men to defend what land they held, with little kindness for strangers. I learned the Fortress of the Sun was now known as the Fortress of Rain, haunted by the undead, and none would venture into the lands covered by the Boa Visk storm. The sorcerers of Dalmora were no help. Desperate, I sought out others. I finally found one who would help me, a warlock in the Carmasta Wastes, near the mountain they call the Black Horn."

Falken frowned. These warlocks and so-called drifting sorcerers were often outside the control of the councils and guilds that controlled magic. They were known for delving into forbidden powers. All his life, he'd been warned to have no truck with them for either knowledge or power. "And what did this Black Horn warlock tell you?"

"Vendle believed the blood moon had wreaked havoc upon the powerful storm spell the Boa Visk had wrought with their arcane magic, sealing a curse upon the fortress and the land around it. Anyone who died within its borders before the curse was broken would have their spirit trapped here as a ghost, unable to move on to the afterlife. He was the only one bold enough to tell me how to break the curse."

Domlen fell silent, turning to stare out the window at the misty drizzle and the gray sky beyond. His eyes were haunted, his mouth drawn, the lines on his rough features even more prominent. He looked nothing like the powerful man who'd captured Falken. Now he seemed a broken man, lost to despair. Again it stirred pity in the prince's heart. Here was a man he should hate...and yet, after all that had happened and all he'd learned, his old hate had faded to nothing.

"The warlock told you the curse could be broken with blood," Falken offered. "Blood to turn his breaking spell powerful enough to end the storm."

Domlen nodded. "Royal blood from a highborn line. If the blood were spilled on the night when the crimson moon reigned supreme in the sky, the curse would lose its ability to feed and sustain itself on Vosk's power. The storm would end. My people's spirits would be freed. All it would cost was the life of one man."

"So you traveled to Teirlan and seized me."

"Not at first, no. I believed there was another way. But Vendle only laughed and called me a fool. He swore that eventually the ghosts would turn. They would lose their humanity and change into revenir."

"Phantoms who steal life-force from the living," Falken said and felt his heart go cold as he thought of how many ghosts had to be trapped in the fortress. "And this many of them...they could devastate entire villages and towns."

"Yes. Even large cities would not be safe from such a large number of them. So I purchased the knife and the accoutrements for the curse-breaking spell from Vendle, along with the binding bracers. Yet, at first I continued to search for a different answer. Time and again, I was turned aside by the learned men of magic. They were busy with their own personal battles or with wars against the Boa Visk. Finally, I returned home to my fortress. The spirits greeted me as though I had merely left for an afternoon ride instead of having been gone for nearly a year. I lived here, after a fashion, surviving on what meager stores remained after the siege. But over time, I began to notice changes in the ghosts. Some began to lose their awareness. Their humanity. I had no more choices and very little time."

"You had to find a king or a prince," Falken broke in. "But with the Tharsgald line ended by the assassination of a king, the country in disarray, and the king's heir locked away in a palace fortress...you had to travel much farther southward. Was there truly ever a jyrdoth drake that I hunted, or was it simply a ruse?"

"A ruse, but it was more luck than guile. I learned that the king of Teirlan had a sorcerer son who was loved for keeping the common folk safe against monsters and demons. A hero, in other words. So I sowed the rumors of the drake and staged some crude evidence in the outlying farms." He shrugged. "The commoners spoke far less kindly of your brothers, so if I could have lured one of them instead, I would have. But it is easiest to lure a hero."

Falken kept all expression from his face, but the man's words touched him in an unexpected way. He wasn't aware that the common people viewed him as such—as a hero and a protector. He didn't think of himself that way. He was a sorcerer, true, and his magic made him powerful. But he envisioned heroes as sword- and lance-wielding warriors, not men who spent much of their time in libraries studying dusty tomes. A hero... To be called such staggered him into speechlessness.

"You know the rest of the tale," Domlen continued. "When you came with the royal guard to investigate the rumors of a drake, I ambushed you and stole you out from under their noses."

"And you intended to sacrifice me last night..."

"I did. Before that, I allowed other blood moons pass while I prepared the spell according to Vendle's instructions. Because even then, I didn't want to go through with it. I hoped there was another way." He shrugged and let out a long breath. "When the hour came, I found I did not have the strength necessary to do what had to be done."

Falken gave him a wry smile. "For that, at least, you have my complete gratitude."

They sat together in silence for a time, until the log on the fire burned low and Falken went to tend to it. As he did, Domlen began to cough again, deep, shaking coughs that appeared as if they hurt him.

Falken moved back to his side. Domlen's expression was closed off again. He'd retreated into his emotionless demeanor, but Falken reached out and took his hand, turning it toward the light so he could better see the blood spattered there. Domlen tried to draw his hand away, but Falken held it tight. It said much about how badly the other man was hurt that he didn't have the strength to pull free.

"When you didn't complete the spell you set in motion, the energy, the mystic force struck at your soul," he said. "It damaged your soul-body bond. The harm was physical and spiritual. It's remarkable you lived at all."

Domlen's face was grim. "What is it you said? I may yet die."

"That's true. Much of what I tried to do was heal that damage, essentially cauterize the spirit-body bond so that it could remain intact. I'm not certain how well it worked."

"I'm feeling stronger already," Domlen said, and he did sound a little better. "You don't owe me or my people anything. In fact, I owe you much and more. When you go, I will not try and stop you."

Falken looked into the other man's storm-gray eyes. His hate and fury at being imprisoned, at being subdued by this man and kept captive against his will, at nearly being murdered by him, all of that toxic emotion had already drained out of him. Now he only felt a deep weariness — an emptiness mixed with sorrow and pity. The stark change was the emotional equivalent of being bucked off by a horse and thrown into a ditch.

Still, he was deeply torn. He wanted nothing more than to put this place, this nightmare behind him forever. After all, what was this place or who were these people to him? Domlen was nothing, a lord of a far-off land ravaged by war and magic. Falken was a prince. He had his own problems back home with the imperial court and with his brothers. But now that Falken had access to his magic again, Domlen clearly expected to be abandoned, even if he no longer feared Falken would kill him in revenge. The lord of the fortress seemed like a broken man, bereft of hope, and it stirred something in Falken's heart.

He leaned forward and touched Domlen's shoulder, trying to reassure him. "I read High Urrian. I'll go to the library and see if any of the books there might show us another way to break this curse. I make no promises, but I shall try. Yet, I *will* promise you one thing. I won't leave you here to die alone."

With surprising strength, Domlen took hold of his arm and drew him closer. Astonished, Falken did not immediately react, even as Domlen lifted himself from the bed and captured his lips in a kiss that sent pleasure flooding through his body. But even as he felt himself responding to the other man's kiss—his heart pounding, his thoughts reeling, his cock growing hard—he suddenly drew backward, breaking that lightning contact between them. He jerked his arm out of Domlen's grip. The lord did not fight him, only watched him with those serious, soulful eyes.

"Never do that again," he snarled, getting to his feet. "You do not have the right."

Domlen closed his eyes and nodded once. He expected the rejection, Falken realized. Perhaps part of him fully believed he deserved it. But despite how strongly Falken's body had reacted to the kiss, this was too soon for him. Especially after he'd deliberately tried to seduce the other man in order to escape. Right now there was too much bad blood between them for thoughts of...anything else.

But when Domlen opened his eyes again, looking away to the window, the man could no longer hide his sorrow and pain. What had changed was that now Falken understood it completely.

So instead of leaving him alone, Falken hesitated on the brink of a decision before finally taking the plunge. "You're hurt, and I'm still not certain how badly. But if you have the strength to drag me into a kiss, then perhaps tomorrow you could show me this library of yours." He held up a hand. "But only if you are feeling stronger. I will help you, so don't attempt the stairs without my aid again."

Domlen smiled. It was as if the sun had finally broken through the storm clouds outside. It lit up the other man's face. Made him handsome, almost beautiful.

Falken knew they would make a foolish sight tomorrow, hobbling down the stairs and through the fortress together. Lord Domlen was large and heavily muscled, the very picture of a warrior, and he would be leaning on Prince Falken, lean and lithe and a handbreadth shorter. But he suspected they could make it all the way to the library, relying upon one another.

As Falken left the tower so Domlen could rest, he realized his lips were warm.

CHAPTER SIX

Perhaps getting out of bed and coming along had been a mistake, Domlen belatedly realized the next day as he and Falken slowly made their way down the corridor to the library. Prince Falken was right beside him, helping support his weight. The prince might not be a large man, but he had good endurance, and not once did he complain about their sluggish progress or how heavy Domlen was to support. In fact, Falken was surprisingly attentive, stopping to rest often whenever Domlen began to flag.

Still, they had picked up an entire entourage of concerned people as they went—servants, Caramore the steward, guards—all of them rushing around and opening doors for them and clearly wanting to help. The prince had tensed when the first person had rushed over to aid them. It happened to be the guard Ronev, Pilla's lover. Falken stared openly at the ghost, but Ronev either didn't seem to notice or didn't seem to mind. Domlen had murmured, "They will not harm you. Not as they are now. They see you as my guest."

After that, Falken had seemed to relax a little. Although he continued to watch the gathering ghosts with wide eyes, and once Domlen heard him whisper, "They seem so very real."

Finally, Domlen, Prince Falken, and their ten-phantom escort entered the library. Falken peered around at the bookcases lining the stone walls and set between large windows. Meanwhile, Domlen felt strangely tense, as if he needed Falken's approval of the library. Which was absurd. He was no librarian, so what did the man's opinion matter to him? But Falken *did* love to read, so books were important to him.

"A respectable library for a stronghold," Falken finally admitted.

"Many of the books were here from ancient days," a quavering voice announced from behind a tower of leather-bound tomes stacked on one of the tables. Then Yosel the Sage stood up from behind his book barricade and smiled warmly at them. "This fastness was not built by the men of Tharsgald, but by the Urrian Re, who were sorcerers of power." All at once he seemed to realize how many people had entered the library along with Domlen and Falken. He blinked at the throng owlishly. "It seems I have quite a party visiting."

Domlen smiled. "We do have a great many mother hens following us about." He glanced at the head steward and nodded. "Thank you for your escort, Caramore. We've arrived safely." He glanced around at the people with them. "You may all return to your duties."

The steward bowed and shooed away the servants. After assessing there were no drakes or deadly zarskon hiding in the library commons, the guards departed as well.

Falken was staring at Domlen openly, but the expression on his face was odd.

"What is it?" he asked, frowning.

The prince shook his head and didn't reply right away. First he helped Domlen to a seat near Yosel. Only when Domlen had his rump safely settled on the chair did Falken step back and finally answer. "Your people love you. It's easy to see."

Domlen felt a flush creep up his neck at the tone of the man's voice: both surprised and admiring.

Yosel laughed gently. "I have served other lords, my young friend. But few as dedicated as Lord Domlen. He truly cares about his people. He would do anything for those in his charge. Highborn or low, it makes no matter."

Now Domlen was blushing. He cleared his throat uncomfortably, but that set off a bout of coughing. Falken put a hand on his arm, staring at him with concern. Domlen gently waved him off.

"You do not look well, my lord," Yosel said, his bright eyes narrowing as he looked Domlen over. "You should be in bed."

"I have no time to lie about like a wastrel," Domlen replied. "Prince Falken asked to see our books. He can read High Urrian."

Yosel's gray, furry eyebrows lifted as he turned to focus on Falken. "Impressive, your highness. I am ashamed to admit, I have not the skill for High Urrian. Isodoran is another matter entirely; I speak it fluently. If you read High Urrian, I take it you are a sorcerer..." He squinted at Falken's face. "From the southern regions, most likely. The Ortelo Kingdom or perhaps Teirlan."

"Teirlan," Falken confirmed with a small smile. He was peering intently at the other man, perhaps searching for the tells indicating the sage was not truly alive. But today Yosel appeared particularly solid, the glow to his eyes very mild, and the cold aura that came from his body was only cool— more like an autumn breeze than a winter gale.

"Ah, I have not had the pleasure of speaking to a denizen of that great nation in quite some time. Welcome to our humble library. I tend the books and dispense wisdom as needed. For that honor, they allow me to rattle around the shelves, left to my own devices." He turned to Domlen and winked. "On occasion our young lord protector will pay me a visit, seeking advice on this or that."

Falken shook his head, his expression amazed. Domlen thought he knew what was coming, but he didn't bother to warn Falken. The prince would have to discover the truth himself and there was no harm in that.

Falken leaned forward, his hands gripping the edge of the table. "Are you aware that you no longer live?"

Yosel was a long time answering. He appeared to be thinking deeply, not upset in the least. "There are times when my thinking...is clearer than at others. At those times, I have memories of what transpired before. When I turn all my power of thought to the matter...then I know. I understand that I am no longer what I once was. But these days I find it difficult to keep the knowledge inside my thoughts." He grinned sweetly. "Age is not kind on the mind or the face." He sighed. "When I saw eighty years, I finally realized the women no longer paid as much heed to my rakishly handsome appearance. Would that I were sixty-nine again..."

Falken laughed and shook his head. Domlen found himself pleased by the sound of the prince's laughter. It was warm, almost boyish. There had been little to smile about and even less laughter in the fortress for years. And the sound of the other man's laughter lightened his heart, made him want to join in.

"So," Yosel prompted gently, moving around the table in the direction of the shelves of books, scrolls, and bound manuscripts. "What might I help you with today?"

The prince opened his mouth to speak, then glanced at Domlen and raised an eyebrow. Domlen hid a smile and nodded for him to go ahead and explain. This man was like no other prince Domlen had ever encountered. He was not timid, but neither did he seem to have the ingrained expectations of royalty. Perhaps Falken was worried about saying too much to the sage. He needn't be concerned. Yosel was as solid as a mountain...and either way, he would forget all he learned here in a few passing days.

"We need all the High Urrian or common tongue volumes on magic or concerning the construction of this fortress, specifically the solartia spells the architects worked into the walls. Also, anything on Vosk, the crimson moon. Oh, and ghosts. We need all the books you have on ghosts."

Yosel's eyebrows shot halfway up his forehead. He stroked his beard and looked from Falken back to Domlen. "Intriguing requests. I would be delighted to help." He stood and gestured for Falken to come with him. When the young prince went to him, Yosel gave him his arm, and together they tottered over to the shelves. Yosel began chattering away on all he knew of the ancient builders of the fortress, while Falken watched him and listened attentively. Domlen smiled, glad they couldn't see his pleasure. The two men together was a sight he found endearing, though he couldn't articulate exactly why. Perhaps because it seemed Yosel had immediately taken on the role of tutor and Prince Falken the attentive student. Or perhaps it was because one of them was a spirit and the other very much alive.

He stayed where he was, slowly rubbing his temple and then massaging his neck, trying to get the pain to fade some. He was still exhausted — weary to the bone in truth — but he was glad he'd come, possible mistake or not. He tried not to feel hope. If Falken didn't discover something in the High Urrian tomes that neither Domlen nor Yosel could translate, that would mean Domlen would be right back where he'd started — desperate to end a curse that would not only destroy his people but turn them into hungry phantoms who would attack the living. He could not think of a worse fate than to see the people he lived with, led into battle, and loved, all turn into something evil.

The despair threatened to take him again. He put his head in his hands, willing away the painful, twisting knot in his throat and the pressure of tears behind his eyes. For his people, he needed to be strong. And he could not show weakness in front of the prince.

Fool. You've shown so much weakness it doesn't matter if you blubber like an infant. Look at you now. Weak. Pathetic. Impotent. Failure —

He forced aside the voice in his head before it could continue its rant. These times were tough enough without him undermining his own spirit. To distract himself, he concentrated on watching Yosel and Falken pull books from the shelves and pile them on a wooden handcart. They already had nearly a dozen stacked there.

Soon he was nodding off, drifting into sleep and then jerking back awake. But it was so warm in the library with the central hearth ablaze. Yosel might be nothing more than a spirit, but he still believed he always felt cold, so he always kept the library fire burning with wood Domlen cut for him...

His thoughts grew fuzzy. Then he remembered no more and only dreamed. Nightmares of the tower and the blood moon and a knife the gods expected him to use upon himself.

* * *

There were nearly a hundred volumes scattered on tables and stacked on the handcart. Falken had been reading through the books since long before noon, but now the light was fading. Though he couldn't see the sun, he guessed evening was quickly approaching.

Yosel was back in the storage rooms, sorting through scrolls and tomes that weren't on the shelves. The oldest and most delicate books and manuscripts were kept in the dry, cool chambers warded against the humidity. Lord Domlen was snoring softly in his chair, his head down and resting on his elbow. The man had fallen asleep early on, but Falken could hardly blame him. He really shouldn't have let the man out of bed in the first place. Then again, he wasn't the man's mother. And Domlen wasn't a man who took *no* for an answer, especially since he was eager for Falken to read the High Urrian texts.

Falken rubbed at the kink in his neck and squinted around at all the open books. At first he'd started skimming indexes, but many of the books were not well organized, though their contents were fascinating. Rare treatises on building and spell crafting that he wished they had inside the Vadolcadium grand library. Still, none of it seemed relevant to the problem of the curse. Before long, his eyes began to ache and his head started to hurt. He was hungry and tired and he suspected he could waste the rest of his life in here, poking around these books without ever finding anything on how to break the curse. He needed at least a dozen or more acolytes working alongside him to help narrow down the search. Trying to do this on his own seemed like an exercise in futility. He simply hadn't counted on there being so much material available.

Domlen was counting on him. Yosel, Pilla, Ronev, and all the other ghosts were counting on him. And his first day had been an abject failure.

He shoved away from the table and slammed both his palms on the wooden surface in helpless frustration. Domlen jerked awake at the sound. Falken grimaced. He hadn't intended to wake the other man, only the sudden impulse to pound something had been overwhelming.

"What happened?" Domlen croaked, his voice rough with sleep. "Another storm?"

Falken shook his head. "Gods forbid we have another rage storm. How many times did lightning strike the tower?"

"Three."

"That is three too many," he said, giving the lord of the fortress a quick look over. More of the man's color had returned, although he had always been rather pale. A hazard, he supposed, of living in a place where the sun never broke free of the clouds. But the sleep seemed to have done him good. Fewer coughs, no blood. Falken was cautiously optimistic.

He swept a hand at the stacks of books. "I could be here a year before finding anything useful," he said, frustration making his voice sharp. "We need to bring more experience to bear on the problem. We need master-level sorcerers. Grandmaster, even. This is beyond me."

Domlen scrubbed a hand across his face, and his palm rasped against his dark stubble. Falken found the man's stubble distracting. He could imagine it would be rough against the skin like sandstone, and when they kissed, it would bristle against him, a little bit of pain with a whole lot of pleasure. Yes, distracting. This was neither the time nor the place for such thoughts. In truth, there *was* no time or place for such thoughts. Ever. Letting go of his anger and bitterness over what had been done to him was one thing, this was…something else entirely.

Domlen watched him with those big, storm cloud-colored eyes. "I begged the grandmasters and high sorcerers for help. I went to every center of magic and learning. They all gave different reasons, but the answer was always no. Only the warlock delivered me a solution, and it was not a pleasant one."

Falken shook his head. "I'm not saying the spell you were given would have failed had you…completed it." He paused again, wondering how much he should explain. "From what I've gathered, it would work. The power of blood magic is potent, even more so when Vosk is alone in the sky. But warlocks can be unpredictable. I've heard tales of some who behaved more like vindictive pranksters. Your warlock might have relished sending you on a mission to bleed dry some royal personage. Two birds with a single stone."

Domlen frowned as if considering it. "I suppose that could be true. I would have no way of knowing. It would be a cruel game to play, however. On both of us."

"Listen," Falken pressed on. "I will go to the Vadolcadium. It has the biggest library and the brightest minds in Teirlan. I'll call a meeting of the high council. They will listen, either to one of their own or to a prince, it matters not. There must be another way to undo this curse."

"You want to go." Domlen said it as a statement of fact, not a question. His tone was devoid of emotion.

"I'm here, the council is in Lindermain. Of course I must go."

"I suppose I have no choice in the matter."

One look in his eyes and it was easy to recognize his fear. Domlen believed he would leave...and never return. Dooming him, and dooming his people.

Falken cocked his head and regarded him evenly. He did not have the patience to reassure the man. Domlen would have to trust him. It wasn't too much to ask after all they'd been through already. "You could wish me luck."

That brought a soft laugh and a smile to the other man's face. "I don't believe in luck."

"You should. It's why you kidnapped me instead of one of my brothers. Believe me, they would never aid you." They would, in fact, never have let Domlen live, especially after he'd collapsed and was completely vulnerable. His brothers were ruthless, sometimes vicious, and could not be trusted. They were one of the reasons he stayed away from court as often as he could.

Domlen met his gaze and held it. "Then luck be with you."

CHAPTER SEVEN

The next morning dawned with a hard rain, hardly a surprise to Domlen. He woke in his chambers to the drumming of water on stone and the lingering memory of a dream. The prince had been in the dream. A terrible storm had raged around them, and he could not remember if he were kissing the man or fighting him. Perhaps both.

He rolled onto his side and stared out the window as the raindrops splashed across the leaded glass. He felt far stronger after another full night's rest. No longer was he coughing up blood, and the pain had faded to a dull roar, easily ignored. It seemed as though he would live, despite his ignorant disregard for the laws of magic.

Even though Falken had escorted him safely to his chambers last evening, the prince had surprised him by choosing to stay in the tower again. "I'm used to it," he'd replied with that wry smile of his. "By now I've broken in the bed the way I want it. Princes are far too lazy to start in again on an entirely different mattress."

Jests aside, Domlen had to admit a growing admiration for the man. He didn't know if he would've been able to sleep again in a room that had once served as his prison, especially after finally gaining his freedom. But the prince did keep the keys with him, making certain Domlen knew it as well. Domlen was hardly in a position to protest. Though he couldn't blame the other man for not trusting him, part of him *wanted* the trust.

They had a long way to go before that. A very long way, if ever.

Prince Falken would leave him, perhaps today, probably on the morrow. Definitely soon. It had only been a fool's hope that the man would stay with him. Almost as foolish as the hope the prince would find a miracle in the stacks of ancient manuscripts, a way to end the curse without sacrificing a life.

The inevitably brought his spirits low. No matter how much Domlen might wish him to remain, he wouldn't. Certainly Domlen no longer had the heart to keep him prisoner, even if that were still possible. The entire thing had been a horrible mistake. A wrong he could never set right. How could he even beg forgiveness? He was not worthy of it and never would be. He had harmed another human being, not a Boa Visk raider or another warrior in battle, but an innocent man. He'd dragged Falken into this nightmare, taken his freedom, taken his magic, almost taken his life…

He heard someone moving about in the main chamber of his quarters. For a moment he wondered if it might be the prince, and his heart did an excited jump. He eased out of bed and drew on some breeches, lacing them up quickly before throwing on a clean tunic. The multiple aches in his body made themselves known, but he gritted his teeth and ignored them. At least he no longer felt as if he were halfway to his death.

When he opened his bedchamber door, he immediately spotted Pilla. The serving girl was standing near the window, facing away from him. In the gloom, she was mostly a darker silhouette against the gray beyond the glass. He frowned as he watched her, wondering why she was here. The ghosts usually did not stray far from the routines of their life, and the chambermaid who cleaned here had always been Dalia. Pilla seemed so intent on something outside that she stood as still as a statue. Goose flesh worked its way up and down his arms, though he couldn't immediately put his finger on the reason why.

When she did not turn to him, he gently cleared his throat. When that still did not get a reaction, he addressed her directly. "Pilla. Is something amiss?"

She didn't answer, didn't even turn his way.

He continued to watch her for another long moment. Then he circled toward her, his hands clammy, his heart beating fast. Something was wrong here. Yet his feet moved him forward of their own accord.

She finally reacted when he touched her shoulder. He'd touched the ghosts before. They did not have flesh as such, but they did have a force, a presence that was solid enough for them to touch things, to influence the world around them. They always felt cold, but she felt far colder than he expected. Touching her was like touching snow.

Pilla flinched and wheeled on him, her eyes widening and glowing brighter. For an instant, she seemed to grow translucent, and her aura washed against him like an unseen wave.

Then in a flash, all those changes vanished and she was only Pilla again. The glow in her eyes muted, her aura withdrew closer to her body, and the chill diminished.

She smiled and did a quick curtsey. "Sorry, m'lord. Did you need something?"

He stared at her, hiding his unease, but she only looked back without guile. "I was curious as to why you are in my chambers."

She glanced around, appearing surprised. "I...I don't know. I'm dreadfully sorry, m'lord. I'm certain there was a reason."

"What is the last thing you remember?"

She faltered, touching her temple and wincing. He waited for her to answer, growing ever more uneasy.

"The moon," she finally replied in a whisper. "The red moon..." She turned back to the window and stared at the falling rain.

"Are you feeling well, Pilla?"

She didn't respond. He braced himself and touched her again. If anything, she felt colder. This time she looked at him.

"Perhaps you should go rest," he said carefully. "I'll tell the steward you aren't feeling yourself."

His words seemed to startle her from her daze. "Yes. I..." She did another curtsey. "By your leave, m'lord. I'm sorry to have bothered you."

He nodded. She left quickly, almost fleeing. He stared at the door after she had shut it, troubling thoughts racing through his mind. The ghosts could not seem to retain the things they learned or memories of events after their deaths for more than a few days—a week at most—although they remembered much from their lives leading up to the fall of the Fortress of the Sun. But Pilla had always seemed one of the more perceptive of the spirits here, asking him about Falken when she'd noticed the prince at the window. But this morning had been disturbingly odd. It was as if parts of her essential humanity were fading...

Then again, the spirits had always been strongly affected by the blood moon. Perhaps that had clouded her mind a little. Either way, he would have to be more vigilant and cautious. He went to the chest where he'd hidden the dagger, the one given to him by the warlock. The one he'd nearly plunged into Falken...

He shook that memory away as he lifted the knife out and put it in a blade sheath he could strap to his lower leg, just above his boot. That way Falken wouldn't see it. He had a suspicion the prince wouldn't be pleased to see it again. He wouldn't have brought it along at all if it weren't for his unease about Pilla and the blood moon curse. The plague knife inflicted overlapping wounds both physical and spiritual. That was one of the reasons why Vendle had sold it to him as necessary for the ritual. So the dagger could harm a revenir, though he prayed to any god good enough to listen that he would never have cause to use it.

He donned his cloak and headed for the tower. After climbing the stairs, he found the prince's room empty. Panic grew in his mind at the possibility Falken had already abandoned him, but he fought it back. The signs were clear that the prince had been here and not long ago. The fire had burned to coals. The bedsheets were clearly slept in and still warm to his touch. Not long ago at all.

It took longer than he expected to finally hunt Falken down—long enough that the panic began to nibble at the edges of his thoughts again. But at last Domlen found him, not in the library or the kitchens but outside on the parapet above the eastern battlements.

"Good morning, Prince Falken," he called as he approached along the parapet. "Please be wary here. The walls were heavily damaged by the Boa Visk."

A gap fifty paces wide had been blasted in the fortress wall. Large piles of rubble were strewn in all directions. There were no physical remains of those who had fallen here in defense of the wall. The Boa Visk had buried their own dead before they'd fled the fortress. As for his people, the ones they had executed…Domlen had buried them all in a mass grave near the southern wing. He had worked alone, in the rain. It had taken nearly a month of continual labor. In the end, he had nearly died of exhaustion and damp lung before he had finished. It was one of the darkest of his memories, and that was saying much.

Prince Falken turned his way at the sound of his voice. That small smile turned up the corner of his lips. "Thank you for the warning, but I do have eyes." He pointed at the jagged and sheared away stone at the gap and at the stress cracks that had spread out from the break. "It's staggering to think how much power they brought to bear on this part of the wall. Despite the hole they blasted, the surrounding stonework is still sound enough. It is a strong fastness. I can understand how, when the solartia still powered the spells, attackers would break themselves on the defenses in vain."

Domlen walked up beside him, feeling pride in the other man's words. Almost as if he had played a role in building the fortress himself, which was utterly foolish, as it predated the rise of Tharsgald. But his flash of pride didn't last. These days, he rarely came to this part of the fortress. Too many memories. The blood and desperation, fighting in the mud and the rain as the storm raged overhead. This place brought the melancholy too close.

Falken noticed his silence. He glanced at Domlen, his brow furrowed. "Will you tell me how you survived?"

"I did not try to survive. I fought like a demon." He pointed below them, to the center of the gap in the walls. "When the wall fell, I made my stand there and met them head-on, with my surviving warriors behind me. We slew many of them, but they were too strong. Once the walls were lost, we retreated to defend the main keep. I was wounded by a Boa Visk blade. Their sorcerers singled me out and bound me with magic so I could not move or fight. My men rallied to defend me, but they were surrounded and killed as I watched, helpless to aid them." His jaw clenched. He felt the churning storm of emotion swelling inside him, straining at the walls he'd erected to keep it back. He touched his chest where the scar was beneath his clothing. "Afterward, they seared my wound closed. Then they made me watch as they sacked the fortress and murdered both soldiers and servants. It did not matter to them."

The prince settled a comforting hand on his shoulder. Domlen met his gaze. At first he thought he saw pity in the other man's eyes and that angered him, but when he looked deeper, he realized it was something far more complex. There was anger there, mixed with a deep sympathy and...respect?

"I apologize," Falken said softly. "It was wrong of me to ask. I should have considered how difficult it would be for you." He withdrew his hand and frowned back at the ruined battlements. "I'm often selfish. Or at least I am when I open my mouth. I blurt out whatever words come to mind, regardless of the consequences."

"No. You deserve to know if you wish to know. I've drawn you into this. I've lost the right to keep secrets from you."

The prince met his gaze again before nodding. Accepting the words. He looked back toward the main keep. "I am hungry though," the prince said, surprising him with the abrupt change in subject. "Join me for a meal?"

"As long as you pay no mind to how it tastes," Domlen replied, and was gratified when the prince laughed.

Together, they headed for the kitchens. Although Domlen was able to walk unaided now, he kept their pace mild. As they moved, he heard the other man's stomach suddenly give a loud, sustained rumble.

Falken glanced at him with a sardonic grin. "I don't suppose you have a nice fatty duck hidden somewhere in this soggy place? Perhaps something you were holding out on, hiding for some celebration or other. Even an apple... I'd scale the outside of that tower with my bare hands for one green apple."

"Are you saying you're bored with the provisions leftover from the siege?" he gently teased. "When they sent me here, I was told it was fare fit for a king."

"They lied to you," Falken said with mock gravity. "Although I suppose a hungry man cannot complain. After we choke down our food, we can return to our research. I want to be sure the answer is not in those ancient books before I set out for Lindermain."

Domlen stiffened. He couldn't help it.

Falken frowned. "Don't worry. One way or another, I will help end this. I will do all that can be done to free your people."

He couldn't respond. There was a knot in his throat, choking him, and he did not trust himself to speak. He didn't dare believe the prince spoke the truth. He didn't feel worthy of hope.

* * *

Falken was certain of one thing: he would never eat salted mutton again in his life. If he were the heir to Teirlan instead of only a third son, he would consider banning it entirely. One of the things he was most looking forward to back home was a decent meal.

Oh, and sunshine, of course. He wouldn't go indoors again for a year.

He was headed to the library with Domlen after their meal. They'd eaten mostly in edgy silence. He didn't know if the tension between them was a result of him asking about the fall of the fortress and making Domlen relive those memories or because he'd announced he would soon be leaving. Yet, the depth of his own anger surprised him. He found himself seething as he gnawed on salty gristle, his mind churning up once again all the wrongs Domlen had done to him. But he was not like his brothers, vindictive, spiteful, always seeking revenge and nursing grievances. He wouldn't be like them—he simply refused. So when these feelings swelled up inside him, he only acknowledge them, understood that he had a right to them, and then he let them go. They would poison him from within if he dwelled upon them. He had chosen not to stain his hands with Domlen's blood. At the same time, Domlen had—when the hour was at hand—refrained from taking Falken's life, despite his belief that it was the only way to save his people. So although Domlen had wronged him terribly, he found it was possible to overcome it, to look beyond and focus his understanding on what had driven the man to such a desperate act.

Still, all was not roses. At times there remained an awkwardness between them, an uneasiness that seemed to gape between them like a chasm. While a good part of him wanted to help bring an end to the tragedy that had swallowed the fortress and consumed Lord Domlen, another part of him wanted to be done with it and away from here forever. That colder part of him maintained that he owed nothing to Domlen or to the spirits trapped here, to the land ravaged by storms, to what might happen if this blood moon curse was not ended. He had his own problems back in Lindermain. He had a father who scarcely valued him, and then only because of his magic, using him like a weapon to hunt down monsters that sometimes wandered into Teirlan from the wastelands beyond the mountains. He had a middle brother who resented him for even being that useful to their father, and his oldest brother mistrusted him because he was the heir but had no magic.

He shook away the conflicting thoughts. The divide inside him wouldn't be resolved any time soon, certainly not during a walk to the library.

Their footsteps echoed down the long corridor leading to the library. Only one lamp had been lit for the entire hallway. The rain hitting the windows made rippling shadows on the opposite walls through the gloom. At first he wondered why the corridor wasn't more brightly lit. Then he realized that, after all this time cut off from the world by the curse with no trade and no markets, the fortress had to be low on all essentials, including lamp oil.

Someone was standing at the farthest window along the hall, near the door to the library. A woman. He thought he recognized her as the serving girl he'd seen from the tower. Her lover had been the guardsman who had followed Domlen into the tower room. Which had been the moment Falken had finally realized there was something deeply wrong with this place.

Beside him, Domlen slowed. He was staring at the serving girl, his face pale, his lips compressed into a tight line.

"What's wrong?" Falken asked.

Domlen didn't respond. Falken wasn't certain the man had even heard him speak. After a moment, they started forward again, approaching the girl. The young woman didn't turn toward them, even as they drew near. She was rocking slowly back and forth and humming a tune to herself. He didn't recognize the melody, but it was soft and haunting enough to raise the hairs on the back of his arms.

"Pilla," Domlen said softly. The girl did not answer and still did not turn. "Pilla, what's wrong?"

"The moon," she whispered, and the sound of her voice sent a chill down Falken's spine.

"Something's wrong with her." He reached out to grab Domlen and stop him from moving too close.

He might as well have been trying to halt a charging bull. Domlen scarcely paused as he approached the girl. "Pilla, can you hear me?"

The serving girl wheeled on them, blindingly fast. As she moved, her body blurred and transformed. What turned to faced them could no longer be remotely mistaken for a human. The girl's eyes glowed red-white, as if they burned like coals, and her pupils could no longer be seen. Her mouth had grown in size until it filled most of her face like a jagged hole. Her skin began to shimmer. The cold coming off her body was as strong as a winter wind. Her limbs were now thin and misshapen, her hands ending in long, blade-like fingers.

Revenir. The thought tumbled through his mind on a wave of fear. Domlen had warned him this would happen—

The revenir lunged at them. Domlen stumbled backward with a cry of shock, knocking into him. The revenir was quick. She sprang at them, leaping higher than any living human could. She came down on Domlen's shoulders, slamming into him with her knees while grabbing his head between both her hands.

Falken expected to see Domlen fall under the force of her attack, but he only took a single step backward in surprise. The revenir's eyes flashed even brighter as she opened her wide mouth and began to draw life force from Domlen. As it left his body, Domlen's life force glowed like a ray of golden sunlight as it passed into her mouth.

"No!" Falken yelled, seizing his magic. His chanted spell hit the phantom with a blast of mystical force and sent her flying through the air.

The revenir didn't seem to have any weight. She effortlessly twisted around in midair, righting herself and floating gently to the floor.

"Run!" Domlen shouted. The revenir was now staring directly at Falken, those red eyes flashing. She hissed like a cat and stalked in his direction. Domlen threw himself in front of her, blocking her path to Falken.

"Get out of the way!" He couldn't use magic if Domlen was between him and the revenir.

Domlen didn't move aside. Instead, he stooped and started fumbling at something near his boot, but the phantom sprang at him again. He swung at the revenir. His fist impacted hard but didn't seem to strike the revenir so much as sink into the surface of its body, as if he'd punched something thick and viscous like jelly. She ignored the blow and wrapped herself around him, clinging like a batleech and trying to siphon away his life force again.

There was no time for hesitation, no time for thought. Falken darted forward and grabbed the revenir around her thin arm. He didn't try to wrench her free with his physical strength. Instead, he released his mage-senses, tuned to the mystical energies that kept the revenir in this world, and sought out the parasitic connection it had formed with Domlen. To his senses, the connection felt like a fiery dagger plunged into Domlen that was simultaneously piercing him and sucking him dry.

He concentrated all his mental power on that connection. With the strength of his will, finely honed from years of study and focus, he ripped it away. The revenir screeched and turned on him again. Before he could react, she thrust her hand into his chest. He felt her fingers, ending with points like knife-blades, pierce his heart.

The pain was mind crushing. His scream rang in the hall, echoing back to him in clearest agony. The revenir drew even closer, hissing eagerly, preparing to steal his life force. The pain broke his connection to his magic, and all spells and thoughts were driven out of his mind by the white-hot flood.

But then Domlen was there, looming behind the revenir. "Forgive me, Pilla," he said, an instant before he drove the green-bladed dagger into her.

The revenir froze, those blazing red eyes going wide, and her mouth gaping open farther than he would've believed possible. She let out a lingering, ear-splitting howl. Then the revenir shattered into thousands of pieces as though she were a mirror smashed by a rock. The pieces crashed to the ground and flashed out of existence.

Falken sank to the cold stone floor. He was panting hard. The pain from the revenir's attack had finally lessened to the point where he could think again, but the only thoughts he seemed able to form were about how much pain he was in. He tried to get back to his feet and fell on his face. He stayed lying on the ground, all his muscles trembling uncontrollably. He thought he might be dying. It certainly felt that way.

Then the world spun as strong arms slid around him and lifted him up. Falken's vision was darkening at the edges, his head pounding, and the roaring in his ears was only growing louder.

"I have you, Prince," a rough and deep voice was saying to him. The arms that held him were like iron; they felt strong enough to hold up the world. He was deeply grateful for that, because it was far warmer in those arms than lying on the cold stone. If he had to die, he wanted to die here, with someone, in their warm arms and not alone on the damp ground.

"You're safe," the voice was murmuring. "Stay with me, my prince, you're safe. I have you."

Those words brought comfort to his pain-hazed thoughts. As his vision went dark and he slipped into unconsciousness, he heard himself whisper, "Thank you…"

And then there was nothing.

CHAPTER EIGHT

Domlen carried Prince Falken cradled in his arms and he plodded through the fortress. He brought the prince to his own chambers because the thought of climbing all those tower stairs when he was still weak twisted his guts into knots. Still, each step was pure pain. The muscles in his arms and back were burning and shaking with strain. His vision became a tunnel. He could only see directly in front of him. He ignored the alarmed exclamations from the servants and guards because he didn't have the breath to waste reassuring them. They couldn't help him anyway.

Please don't die, he thought, grinding his teeth against the weariness working on him. The words became a chanted prayer for Falken inside his head. *Please don't die. Please don't die.*

Falken's skin felt cold and clammy. He hadn't stirred since shortly after Domlen had picked him up and that terrified him. He was responsible for this. Pilla had been the first ghost to turn into a revenir, but he'd feared something was wrong with her after he'd come across her in his chambers. He'd been waiting for this to happen, dreading it. And now it may have cost an innocent man his life. Even though he'd tried to protect the prince, it hadn't mattered. Everything he'd done had gone astray. He'd brought the knife, but he'd hidden it from Falken, so it hadn't been easily at hand when the revenir attacked.

And then there was poor Pilla. Was her soul finally at rest? Or, as he feared, had he destroyed her soul when he'd used the dagger against the revenir? Guilt flooded him. He was drowning in it. Everything he did brought more guilt crushing down on his shoulders. Pilla, and now Falken.

Again Falken.

No. The prince couldn't die. What would be left? Nothing. His last hope of freeing his people from this nightmare curse would be done and gone. He would have the blood of an innocent man on his hands...and he wouldn't even have broken the curse. It was the worst of both worlds.

He kicked open the door to his chambers and hurried inside. A chill wracked him when he glanced at the place he'd seen Pilla staring out the window. He'd feared something was wrong...and he hadn't acted.

Falken groaned and shifted a little in his arms. Domlen's heart leaped, hoping the man was regaining consciousness. He brought the prince into his bedchamber, settled him gently on the bed. The prince shifted again and muttered something Domlen didn't understand because it seemed to be in another language. His skin appeared so pale. Domlen placed a hand on his forehead again—cold and clammy. Then he unlaced the man's tunic so he could examine the place where the revenir had struck him. The flesh on Falken's chest was smooth and unmarked. Whatever harm the revenir had done, it had been damage to his spirit, not his body.

He brought the covers up and tucked them around the prince. Then he went to the fireplace and carefully stacked wood, kindling, and tinder on the iron grate and used flint and steel to spark it alight. Soon he had the fire going strong. He returned to Falken's side, but the prince hadn't moved again, and his breathing had grown shallower. Pacing didn't help, but he did so anyway until a knock at the door distracted him.

When he answered it, he discovered Ronev standing in the corridor.

"My lord," Ronev said, bowing. "I am sorry to trouble you. But I have nowhere else to turn."

"It is no trouble," he said carefully, praying this had nothing to do with Pilla but certain that was the case. "What is amiss?"

"It's Pilla, my lord. I cannot find her. No one has seen her. I fear the Boa Visk…may have taken her. She's nowhere in the fortress. Could she have gone out beyond the walls?" He shook his head forcefully, his handsome features drawn and worried. "I can't believe she'd be so foolish with an enemy army at our gates."

It was always the same when he dealt with the spirits trapped here. This mix of their thoughts blending with what was currently happening and with pivotal events in their past. The Boa Visk were long gone, but to Ronev, they still besieged the fortress, even though there was no evidence to support this.

"I'm sorry, Ronev," he said, holding the other man's gaze. Those softly glowing eyes were full of worry. "I have not seen her. But I know she would not stray beyond the walls. She's a bright girl, with a good head on her shoulders. I'm certain she will turn up soon." The lie came out smoothly, although he felt as if his tongue had turned to acid inside his mouth.

He hated himself for that lie.

Ronev was crestfallen. "If you do see her, I beg you to tell her to find me right away. And thank you, my lord."

Domlen nodded, watching as Ronev walked away through the gloom of the hallway. He closed the door gently, heartsick and devastated by what had just happened. Ronev's spirit could never forget her. He would relentlessly continue searching for her throughout the fortress forever.

Or until the curse was finally broken.

He shut the door and leaned against it. If someone had stabbed him clean through the heart with a blade, it would've hurt him less than lying to Ronev. But if he had told the truth, he would've crushed the man...until the information faded from his memory in a few days, and he came looking for Pilla once more.

He rested his head against the door panel as hot tears spilled from his eyes, burning along his skin like fire. Weeping would give him no relief. He loathed himself for showing this emotion when it could not change anything. So he took a deep, shuddering breath, squared his shoulders, and crushed all the sorrow and pain deep inside himself where he didn't have to see it. He wiped away the tears with his sleeves. Then he went back into his room to sit by the prince's side.

"I suppose turnabout is fair play," the prince said weakly the moment Domlen entered. "I saved you, you saved me. Makes us even. For now."

Domlen rushed to the bed. He wanted to touch the other

man, for reassurance, for comfort, for what, he didn't know. But he held back, suddenly uncertain if his touch would be appreciated or reviled.

"Don't waste your strength on your japes," he chided, unable to hide his grin. "How are you feeling?"

"Considering that a ghost just turned into a monster ghost and tried to murder me, I'm feeling very well, thank you for asking." He blinked slowly and turned to look at the fire. "That fire feels like heaven." The firelight painted his face in soft oranges, making him beautiful. He looked Domlen straight in the eye. "I'm sorry about the serving girl. Pilla? Was that her name?"

Domlen nodded, fighting to hold all his sorrow in, not letting any grief or despair or worry slip out. Right now Falken needed him strong and supportive. He couldn't let the prince discover how desperate he truly was.

They were quiet for a time. The only sound was the patter of rain and the crackling of the flames. He felt as if there were too much to say between them and yet he had no idea where to begin. For the moment, he was determined to be content that the prince had woken and seemed stronger than he'd dared hope...

"The warlock was right," Falken said, jerking Domlen out of his thoughts. "The spirits trapped here will eventually turn into revenir unless we break the curse."

"This morning, I found Pilla in my quarters. She was at the window, staring out at the rain. She kept mentioning the red moon. When I spoke to her, she seemed dazed, as if lost in a dream."

Falken's expression was grave. "You are a lucky man. She was likely starting to turn and was drawn to the closest life force. Perhaps some part of her still remembered you and she held the hunger back." He shook his head, clearly troubled. "You knew something was wrong. That's why you brought the blade."

"I feared she was close to lost...but I didn't want to give up hope. I brought the knife in case I was wrong."

"You didn't want me to see it." A slight smile turned up the prince's lips. "I thank you for the courtesy, but I am made of stronger stuff than that. The sight of a blade won't turn my knees to pudding, even if it had been at my throat once."

Domlen nodded. He wouldn't admit it aloud, but when he'd first learned he would need to kidnap a member of royalty to break this spell, he'd been laboring under quite a few assumptions about what a member of a royal line would act like. He was continually surprised by Prince Falken, and appropriately taken to task for those assumptions.

"Will you be able to travel to Lindermain to speak to the sorcerers there?" he asked, very aware that, for him and for his people, time was running out.

"I'm not certain I have the strength for travel. Not yet, anyway. Especially not by foot. Do you still own a horse?"

Domlen shrugged. The Boa Visk had slaughtered every animal within the walls for meat when they'd overrun the fortress, including many fine horses. Later, he'd purchased a horse and covered wagon for his journey southward. After Domlen abducted the prince, he'd kept the prince bound and gagged in the back of the wagon for the entire trip back to the fortress. "After we returned, I let the horse out to graze. I feed him what hay we still have left, but he comes and goes through the breach as he pleases. He is yours, if we can find him."

"I thank you, although I'm not certain I could even ride yet. We could take the wagon again. We could go together."

Domlen met his gaze, his heart beating harder. The words had surprised him. He was very aware that the prince was watching him intently. A sudden tension grew in the air between them, but it was unlike any before. The offer staggered him and simultaneously lifted his heart, helping him throw off some of the shadow darkening it after seeing Ronev searching in vain for the person he loved. That the prince would even offer after all Domlen had done to him...the kindness, the generosity — no, the *forgiveness* of it was staggering. It was more than he'd ever hoped to see and far more than he deserved.

And yet, he could not go.

He tried a gentle smile, but it felt strained and sad. "I would be honored. I thank you from the bottom of my heart for the offer. But...I cannot leave my people again. I have the knife. I must stay here and stop them if they turn. If I can't free my people, I must stay here to protect the surrounding lands from the revenir."

Prince Falken only nodded, though there was disappointment in his eyes. "When I am strong enough to travel, I will go. Until then, I will stay with you and search the old texts in your library for anything that might help."

He bowed his head in gratitude. "Thank you. I would be in your debt."

After that, he stood to go, intending to bring in more firewood and refill the pitcher of water from the wells. Instead, he paused and looked down at the prince. He almost didn't ask, but in the end, his need to know was too strong.

"Did I destroy her? Did I keep Pilla from the afterlife and damn her to nothingness?"

Prince Falken reached out and took his hand, giving it a firm squeeze. "I'm sorry, Domlen. I don't know the answer. I pray she's found peace. If the gods are good, she is at rest."

Domlen nodded and left. He did not say that long ago he'd stopped believing in the goodness of the gods.

* * *

Falken was lucky to be alive and knew it. Two full days had passed since the revenir attack. He was lying on Domlen's bed with his hands clasped behind his head, staring at the stone arches supporting the ceiling, feeling better in body but tired in soul.

Witnessing the transformation of Pilla from the love-struck serving girl he'd first spotted stealing kisses from her lover to the savage and relentless phantom that had attacked them on the way to the library had hit him with the force of a punch. It changed things for him. Perhaps he could never fully understand the position Domlen found himself in, but it seemed clearer in Falken's mind now. He could understand the desperation and the fear, knowing the curse would transform his people into revenir. Knowing those revenir would go in search of life force to consume in a vain attempt to quell their unending hunger. Innocent people would die.

Falken was a prince, but he was not heir to the throne. While he considered the people of Teirlan his subjects, it was only in the most abstract of ways — as if they belonged more to his family line than to him personally. With two brothers ahead of him in the line of succession, it was unlikely he would ever be king, especially as his oldest brother would be marrying in the coming summer. Then his brother's heirs would stand to inherit. Long ago he'd made his peace with that. But now he was looking at things in a different light. What if it were *his* people trapped in a nightmare curse that would not only destroy them, but destroy the people around them? And not simply faceless subjects who owed him fealty, but people he knew by name. People that he'd known for years, if not his entire life. What would that change for him? Would he have kidnapped Domlen and sacrificed him to end the curse had their positions been reversed?

He couldn't answer that. No, he didn't *want* to answer that. And yet such was the situation Lord Domlen found himself in. Could he forgive the man, after putting himself in his boots and walking those miles? The answer was…not yet. The things done to him were still too close. The wounds too raw. But given time…

Domlen arrived with breakfast a few minutes later. His stomach growled, even though the food was still the same slop he'd been eating since his arrival. At least it was hot and there was enough of it. He found it easier to be grateful, especially after nearly dying. After enough time passed, he knew he'd go right back to complaining about the lack of warm, fresh bread and butter, roasted duck, and squash drowning in cream sauce. His stomach rumbled again. He definitely wasn't helping matters by thinking about various court dishes he was missing out on.

"How are you feeling?" Domlen asked as he set the serving tray down within Falken's reach. Nearly every time he entered the room, he asked the same thing. It would've been annoying, but Falken could tell from the man's expression that he truly cared. Domlen was worried. And it wasn't simply because his chance at a ransom was endangered or he would lose the key component to breaking the curse. Domlen simply cared.

He didn't know how to feel about that. Usually the man was so closed off and emotionless that Falken had trouble getting a glimpse of his feelings. Since the attack, however, Domlen hadn't seemed as distant. He certainly was attentive.

"I'm feeling stronger." He pushed himself into a sitting position and stretched.

The other man hesitated and then nodded once. His expression closed down again like a portcullis slamming shut. There, Falken had gone and praised the man for crawling out of his shell and as soon as he thought it, the man went and proved him wrong.

"Not strong enough to risk leaving yet," he continued, in case that was why Domlen had gone cold. "I need to spend more time with the texts here before heading south. There are arcane books here that are not at the Vadolcadium. If the answer *was* here all along, and I missed it..." He shook his head, not bothering to continue. He'd gone back and forth in his mind about whether he should leave at once or spend precious time sifting through the High Urrian manuscripts and scrolls in the fortress library. Right now, he didn't have much choice. He was tired of lying on his back all day. The revenir hadn't killed him, but going stir-crazy might just finish him off.

"Eat first," Domlen said. "You need to keep up your strength. Then we'll go to the books."

"You would make an excellent mother, Lord Domlen."

"Get buggered," the other man growled.

They stared at one another. Then Falken laughed. And Domlen, gods be good, actually smiled.

Later at the library, Yosel brought him some of the oldest scrolls and texts in the fortress. They carefully unrolled them and stretched them on a table, using steel weights to keep the edges down. Meanwhile, Domlen had paced around the room until Falken ordered him to go find something useful to do because his constant pacing was distracting. Yosel voiced his full support. So with a parting glower, Lord Domlen had finally left them to work in peace.

He'd been wearing that dagger, though. Despite Falken's bold words to the contrary, the sight of the blade in its sheath sent chills down his spine.

Soon enough he put it out of his mind again. Most of what he read had little to do with what he sought—some keystone element that would either break the energy chain feeding the curse or would allow the spirits trapped here to escape bondage and find the afterlife. Instead, he sifted through treatise on war craft, works on raising horses and animal husbandry, crop rotation, books on astronomy and divination. Books of history for all the surrounding kingdoms and some of lands that no longer existed. He lost several hours poring over one scroll that contained the original plans for the fortress and detailed descriptions of how the solartia spells in the walls had worked. The builders had expected the fortress to be well-nigh invincible for as long as the sun continued to rise. Unfortunately, they hadn't been correct.

The sun was setting somewhere behind the wall of gray rain when Yosel finally placed a hand on his arm to get his attention. The old man had lit several lamps to help stave off the gloom, but Falken realized he'd been squinting and leaning closer and closer to the scroll he'd been examining.

"Perhaps we should call it a day, good prince," Yosel suggested. "The darkness grows too thick for these old eyes, and you must be hungry."

He realized he *was* hungry again, which he took as a good sign. After he'd first woken from the attack, his appetite had largely vanished, crowded out by pain and bone-deep weariness.

"That's probably best," he grudgingly admitted. Part of him wanted to stay and continue searching, but the rest of him was tired—more tired than he first realized—and hungry. His neck was sore, and he had a bit of a headache from the eyestrain. He carefully began to roll up the parchment and set it aside.

"If you must return tomorrow," Yosel said, "and I suspect you must, it might be most efficient to leave the books and scrolls where they are. Then you may immediately begin again from where you left off."

He nodded and smiled. That was a tiny bit of weight off his mind. The head librarian in Lindermain would have a seizure if even a royal prince left this scale of mess on a table in the grand library. He found he rather liked Yosel. He wished he would have met the man when he'd still lived...

Yosel seemed to misread his look. "Do not worry about me, good prince. I will tend to the lamps, the fire, and the books. These days I find I do not have much sleep in me. It is no bother to look after things."

"I suppose it would be pointless to feel guilty about leaving this mess behind when I'm only going to make it again tomorrow," he replied, waving a hand at the disordered stacks of books, bound manuscripts, and scrolls. He glanced at the door and then hesitated. He hadn't yet been alone with any of the ghosts in the fortress. This was the first time he could chance asking whatever he wanted.

What he chose to ask surprised him. "How long have you known Lord Domlen?"

The old man smiled softly, staring at the ceiling and stroking his beard as he searched his memory. Yosel so perfectly fit the image of the wise old man—philosophers, sorcerers, and alchemists—that Falken had to grin.

"The young lord came to The Fortress of the Sun perhaps eight years ago. He was appointed by the Great Lord Dysiah, the Warden of Korsdale, under the decree of King Leovic of Tharsgald. Lord Domlen was charged with holding the northern passes at any cost. This was back when the Boa Visk were still a far away rumor. They had not yet overrun any of Tharsgald or turned the lakelands into utter desolation. He was…very intense, our young lord."

Falken smirked. "Not much has changed."

Yosel chuckled lightly. "Oh, appearances can be deceiving. He did not fit in all that well at first. He believed this place was a backwater, isolated and ignored, where lords unpopular with the court were sent to fade away, far from any place they could make trouble."

"Having spent my fair share of time dealing with court intrigues, that does not seem beyond the bounds of believability."

"No, no, he was quite right. Lord Domlen Jadale was problematic for the king. He was a talented general and leader of men, but the Jadale line once carried the blood of kings. The Jadale dynasty lasted for over a hundred years, until invaders from the south conquered the land. Sandsenta Jadale was the king who yielded, bending the knee and swearing fealty to the new rulers." Yosel's gaze was razor sharp, so bright and cutting that it momentarily stunned Falken. "They were from Teirlan. In time, this lesser house of the Fettengald line rebelled, breaking from Teirlan and raising a new kingdom."

Falken was speechless. His ancient ancestors had actually warred and conquered Tharsgald, taking it from Domlen's ancestors? Then they'd lost it again because of a rebellion? Not only was Domlen a highborn lord, but he had the blood of kings? "Does Domlen know about his family history?"

"Hmm. Hard to say. We've never spoken of it. I have never heard him mention it, though he is very aware his father was a highly regarded general who fought wars across the Green Salt Sea. His father was killed on one such campaign years ago. I happen know about his bloodline because it was my business to know, both when he arrived and afterwards. The court was clear they wanted an eye kept on him and were not coy about the reasons why. Long had it been feared that some scion of the Jadale line might rise again in rebellion. But in time, they forgot about him, which is what they wanted. And in time, I came to love him like a son. Which wasn't what they wanted, but by then they no longer cared. The troublesome problem of Lord Domlen was gone, and that was all they needed."

"Why did they fear him? Would Domlen ever rise in rebellion?"

Yosel snorted derisively. "You've met the man. He is dedicated to his duty beyond all measure. He would not betray his trust or those who entrusted this place and these people to him. Though at first he was bitter about it, he came to love the Fortress of the Sun and her people. Her *family*, if I should be so bold as to speak my true mind." He sighed. "But at times it weighed upon my spirit. That he cannot read the language of his distant ancestors, but you, a Teirlan prince, can read them...I find that a cruel jest of the gods." His smile was bitter, and his gaze knowing. "But then, there have been many cruel things done here in these later years, is that not true? Cruelty is a snake eating its own tail and growing ever fatter."

"If you knew, why didn't you tell him?"

"Why further burden a man already carrying so many? What would it have gained him to know how hundreds of years ago, one of his great forefathers ruled this land as king? Those times are long gone, ancient history. While his line retained nobility and wealth, their power and standing has much waned with passing generations, until they would've been unrecognizable to their forefathers today."

Falken leaned back in his chair, his thoughts spinning in his mind like a whirlwind. He gave a weak smile, but inside, he felt sick and cold all the way through. "I suppose you are right. What could it change?"

"But now you know the truth and you are his friend. Will you tell him?"

The word "friend" surprised him. He began to wonder if he'd been wrong about how wise this man truly was. Perhaps he was blind. Or losing his wits with age. There was even the chance that being a ghost diminished the powers of perception and thought. Any of those were more likely than this claim of "friend."

But that was beside the point. The question stood. Would he tell Domlen the blood in his veins was royal? If he told the man, what would he do? Falken shook his head. That was a dangerous question.

"No," he answered quietly. "I will not tell him."

CHAPTER NINE

After Falken and Yosel ordered him out of the library, Domlen had been too restless to relax and too nervous to eat. He found himself pacing the battlements, his cloak drenched, cold and wet, with a view of the muddy-brown Loredine River. The river had once been almost crystalline in its clarity, but was now so full of constant soil runoff that it more closely resembled fast-moving mud. His thoughts were chaotic. Full of the prince, full of worry, laced with hope they would find a way to end the curse, while his heart remained heavy with uncertainty. He could not shake off those doubts.

As he waded across the cold, ankle-deep water flowing in a torrent for one of the fortress's drains, an idea suddenly struck him. It was something to occupy him while he waited and paced, unable to help with Falken's research because he didn't speak the needed language. He hated feeling useless.

And to him, being powerless to do something was as horrendous as choking on jagged pieces of bone. He'd never felt more helpless than when the Boa Visk had held him prisoner and forced him to watch the destruction of his people. Nightmares of that time still woke him in a cold sweat, shaking and sick.

He tore his mind away from those thoughts. He needed to stay focused on his idea for the prince. He even began to smile before doubt caught up with him and made him grit his teeth with worry. What if Falken refused? What if he threw the offer back in Domlen's face, spitting scorn? It would be his right, but it would crush Domlen all the same.

No. He refused to be cowed or intimidated by his own fears, refused to knuckle under to self-doubt. He was the lord of this fortress. He had faced battle. He had stood at the breach and defied the monstrous Boa Visk. He could do this.

It took him the rest of the day to set everything up exactly as he wanted it. He was surprised at how excited he was as he worked. By the time it was dark, he was finally ready. He went in search of the prince and found him sitting in Domlen's chambers.

The prince glanced his way and seemed rather subdued. "I was about to head to the kitchens to see about preparing our daily portion of slops," he said. "After spending all day reading, I'm famished."

His heart was beating faster and his mouth was dry when he said, "I would be honored if you would join me for dinner."

Falken hesitated, frowning slightly at the formal tone. "Perhaps I misremember, but don't we usually eat together of late?"

"We do," Domlen said. "Now if you will follow me...?"

He swept a hand toward the door and raised his eyebrows, waiting with his heart in his throat and hoping the prince would not refuse him.

A slow smile spread over Falken's face. "Oh, I love a good intrigue. I suppose you won't say where we are going?"

To that, Domlen only gave him his best mysterious smile.

"I guessed correctly," Falken said with a laugh. "Well, then. Shall we go?"

"Bring a cloak."

"So, somewhere through the rain, I take it?" He immediately held up a hand. "No, don't answer. You've captured my interest. I need to be content and await the big reveal." He arched an eyebrow and his mouth twisted into a small, wry smile. "Unless you're planning on locking me in some dungeon..."

It took all Domlen's self-control, finely honed after years of command, to keep from flinching. Not because he actually planned on harming the man or tricking him into a dungeon cell of course, but because those words brought back all his guilt for abducting the prince and bringing him into this nightmare. Falken's flat-out statement brought back all the antagonism that had spanned between them. Captor and captive. Warden and prisoner. Kidnapper and victim. He could feel his ingrained instinct to withdraw taking over, urging him to take cover behind his internal walls, to don his protective armor. To keep himself wary and defend with cold, emotionless courtesy.

The instinct was strong and it nearly won. But instead, he decided to walk a different path. He might not be a peer to this member of royalty, but there was an undeniable connection between them, forged by what they'd experienced, good and bad, right and wrong. He could not have said whether that connection, as it stood, was noble or bane. Yet, he deeply wanted it to be a good and true thing.

So instead of withdrawing into the persona of the lord of the fortress with all its cold civility, he tried a smile. "If the good prince truly wishes, we can tour the dungeons to his heart's content. They are half flooded and full of slime, mold, and rusting chains, although I believe the rats have all drowned." He sketched a small bow. "Yet, I live to serve. If your highness wishes to experience them in all their glory, we shall make it happen."

"Gods above us, Lord Grim Statue just made a jest. And I swear that was a smile. A smile that didn't show any teeth, perhaps, but I'll happily note it as an improvement."

As he spoke, the prince was shaking his head and grinning. The tension charging the air between them eased.

"In truth, the surprise is nothing of note," Domlen added, trying to sound nonchalant. "It wasn't my intention to build up anticipation."

Falken gave a good-natured shrug. "These days, I believe any change is a good change, no matter how minor. Lead on then, Lord Domlen."

But instead of leading, Domlen and the prince walked together, side by side, through the halls. The servants bowed to them as they passed. He knew they were watching as they made their way up the corridors. Idly, he wondered what was going through their minds. And then a darker part of him wondered if any of the ghosts were thinking of the blood moon...and hunger...

He dismissed those thoughts as he and Falken donned cloaks, grabbed lanterns, and headed out into the storm. Night had fallen. The low clouds were dark and roiling in the sky, but he was glad to see there was no lightning, only rain.

Although he wished he could bring Prince Falken somewhere they could both see the sun.

Falken kept his thoughts to himself as they crossed the courtyard through the sheet of water on the flagstones, rippled by the constant raindrops. They entered the tall tower where he'd held Falken prisoner. It was a risk, bringing Falken here after what this place must mean to him, even though the prince chosen to stay here after he was no longer a captive. Tonight would be a little bit different. This was the highest spot in the fortress, nearly doubling in height any other tower or battlement, so he'd taken the risk.

He turned to the prince. "Do you feel strong enough to climb the stairs?"

"If you can do it, I can do it." Although it was clear from the man's face he held no love for the stone staircase spiraling around the tower.

They dripped their soggy way up the steps to the topmost level. The prince made as if to enter the tower room, but Domlen only shook his head and indicated they should take the stairs to the tower battlements.

The prince's eyebrows rose in surprise, but he asked no questions. He followed the last curving set of stairs, pushed open the trapdoor, and climbed out to where Domlen had erected a makeshift tent across half of the tower top, protecting it from the rain. He'd used oilcloth, tied the guy ropes around the crenel fortifications, and used spear hafts for the corners to keep the whole thing upright. He used a longer pole arm haft for the center, to give the tent roof a slope so it wouldn't collapse in a huge puddle of water. The entire setup would probably blow over in a strong breeze, but for now it was keeping the top of the tower dry. He'd brought up two chairs and a brazier for heat and light. The rubble he'd hauled up from the breach in the wall had been carefully arranged in a circle, forming a crude fire pit. He'd cut a small flap in the overhead oilskin to vent smoke. Finally, there was a small wooden table to the side with a serving dish, the best crystal glasses the fortress still had, and two of the finest bottles of wine from the cellars. Well, the finest of the few remaining bottles not pillaged or broken by the Boa Visk. A dark red vintage from the Huso Valleys and a white from Teirlan.

Domlen didn't look at the prince. He couldn't. Instead, he walked to the brazier and busied himself checking the coals. They were still giving off a decent amount of heat and glowing a deep orange-red.

"You did this for me?" Falken asked from behind him.

The other man's words were soft, his tone gentle. Still, Domlen's heart began beating hard. He clenched his fists so neither he nor Falken could tell if they were shaking.

"I did," he said, then risked a glance behind him.

Falken was not smiling. The expression on his face was...thoughtful, perhaps even pensive. But relief flooded through him when he realized the look in Falken's eyes was warm—pleased. The nervous tension eating away at him throughout the walk here vanished.

"Thank you," the prince said and went to stand next to him by the brazier. He looked at the fire pit built of rubble and then back at the wine and the serving dish. "I see you thought of everything."

"There's one more thing." Domlen went to the serving dish and removed the cover. Inside there were two plates with salt pork in a dark gravy—no mutton here. There were three thin carrots and four tiny red potatoes. And for each of them, half an onion soaking in the gravy.

These were the absolute last of the non-pickled vegetables

in the storage cellar and he'd had to scrounge to find them. And the salt pork...he'd been saving that little treat in the larder for the day he broke the curse.

The prince's entire face lit up with joy at the sight of the meal. His stomach loosed a rumbling growl, and both of them laughed in surprise.

"Sounds like we have thunder to go along with the rain," Falken said as he quickly pulled off his wet cloak, tossed it aside, and hurried to the food. He picked up a piece of the pork with a bit of the potato and gravy and popped it in his mouth. The resulting groan sounded almost sexual in its intensity.

Domlen was no skilled cook. In truth, he'd only learned to prepare basic meals for himself when he'd been on the road, seeking answers about the curse. But seeing the prince as excited as he was to have different food, even if it were meager fare, warmed him to the bone.

The prince handed him a plate and cutlery before taking the other plate for himself. "No more wasting time." He nodded at the chairs beneath the tent. "Join me?"

"Yes."

* * *

There was something about food that healed, Prince Falken decided as he used the last of his potato to mop up gravy. Food replenished the body and healed the spirit. Sharing a meal with another person was an act of intimacy, a closeness that mended wounds. He chuckled to himself and shook his head as he chewed. Listen to him. A few weeks without a decent meal and he became a philosopher of cuisine and the state of the soul.

Domlen turned his way, an eyebrow raised. "What is it?"

"Only a few surprising thoughts." He set his plate aside and leaned closer to the brazier, loving its dry, blazing heat. Dry heat was another thing he'd come to appreciate after all this time in all this wet and damp. He took another sip of his wine. He'd indulged in quite a bit already. Perhaps that was why he'd drifted into philosophy. Wine sometimes made him thoughtful, other times melancholy.

But he felt good. For the first time in months, even before Domlen had kidnapped him, he felt truly good. Yes, he'd had far finer meals prepared by those who studied the art. And yes, he'd just finished a meal with the man who had abducted him from his life of wealth and luxury and brought him to this rain-swamp nightmare. Yet his belly was full, he had a glass of wine in hand, and there was plenty of heat coming from the flames in the fire pit to keep the chill at bay. Oh, and let no one forget, he had his magic back. He idly rubbed the spot on his right forearm where the bracer had been locked on him.

Domlen noticed. His expression was somber as he quietly said, "Share your thoughts?"

Falken had never backed away from a chance to speak, often and at great length, as some of his friends and past lovers would have chided him. He knew the tendency to be loquacious came with being a member of the royal family. His brothers, if anything, were worse. His father could hold forth for hours, boring half the court into a stupor. The other half of the court consisted of retainers too busy practicing the honored tradition of being lickspittles and obsequious toadies. Gods, he did hate the court.

He realized Domlen was still waiting for him to speak. "My apologies. I was brooding over how much I loathe the court...and especially my brothers." He sipped his wine. "Perhaps hate is too strong a word. 'Intense disregard' may better describe my opinion."

The corner of Domlen's mouth quirked upward. "How did that come to pass?"

"A series of a thousand little slights and insults and betrayals. You may find this hard to believe, but I am not one to grind the axe of a grudge. But even when we were kids, I was considered the runt. The third son, who stood little chance to inherit the throne. They used to pull vicious pranks on me, torment me, sometimes they'd give me a beating for no good reason."

"Your father did nothing?"

He shrugged and sipped more wine. It truly was a delightful flavor. From Teirlan, around Red Hill City perhaps. "My father believed that each of us had to be strong. I went to him in tears once, but he only stared at me with those cold eyes and told me to act like the son of a king and stop my womanly bawling. He told me to become a warrior if I wanted to protect myself, but that I should count on no one else to intercede for me."

"Did you? Take up the sword, I mean?"

"I have no talent for blade-play. Or the longbow. Not the crossbow either. But a few years later, about when my testicles dropped, I discovered a talent for magic. For the primal forces of the hidden world."

Domlen's face was inscrutable. "Magic is connected to testicles dropping?"

"It seems that way. For males, anyhow." He waved the notion away. "The point is, once I began training at the

Vadolcadium to become a sorcerer, my brothers stopped the fistfights and pranks."

"Perhaps they grew out of it."

"No, they simply switched to court intrigues. I'll have to deal with my brother, Tobias, becoming king some day, and he doesn't particularly care for me." He swirled his wine in his glass, staring at the rain pattering on the tower roof and running in streams to the drain holes at the base of the crenels. "That isn't rare in our family, though. My father was not pleased to learn I preferred the company of men. He wanted to marry me to the daughter of one of his highborn retainers. To bind the man's loyalty to him. He may still try and force me to marry her." He glanced at Domlen and grinned. "He can't be happy I've disappeared. Not because he misses me, but because it ruined his schemes."

"Would you?" Domlen asked, his tone hesitant. "Marry at your father's command?"

"Why do you think I keep busy away from Lindermain and the palace as much as possible? My studies at the Vadolcadium give me ample excuse to be gone, and even when I'm called to court, there's always this to be done, that to be handled. A recent example, I was dispatched to the north to investigate a rumor about a jyrdoth drake." He glanced around him theatrically. "And look how that turned out."

They were quiet for a time, the only sound the patter of the rain on the oilskin tent and the stone. Domlen went and checked the coals in the brazier again, then filled both their glasses and sat down once more.

"My father never knew that I did not wish to marry a woman," Domlen said. "He was killed when I was young." His mouth tightened in what might've been a smile. "Before my all-important balls dropped."

Falken raised his wine glass. "To balls."

Domlen stared at him for a long moment. Then he shook his head and actually laughed. It was a sound the prince found he rather enjoyed. Deep, somewhat restrained, but far better than the usual grim Lord Domlen. He even raised his glass in answering toast.

"Go on," Falken prompted, curious to discover he really did want to learn more about this man.

"There is not much else to tell. My father died on campaign in Balheim. My mother raised me with the help of my aunts and uncles in Lev-Nacadia, where our family seat had always been. She knew I did not wish to marry a woman."

Falken frowned, judging much from his tone. "It did not please her."

He shook his head. "She wanted grandchildren. An heir. But I have a younger brother. She turned most of her attention to him. I suppose she pinned most of her hopes on him as well, for grandchildren at least." He frowned. "I was at court in Chordlavaq, and she was still trying to arrange a marriage for me, even then. Then the king gave me this commission. With a decree, he made me lord of the Solarahold, Fortress of the Sun. As fancy as the title sounded, the place was notorious as a backwater where undesirables were sent to pasture. In other words, to keep them out of trouble and far from court intrigues."

Falken smiled. "Yosel told me you had a difficult time when you first arrived." He actually found it endearing. It humanized the other man a little. Made him seem less like one of those empty suits of armor standing guard in the corridors. "But you involved in court intrigues? I find that surprising. My brothers revel in them, but I find them odious. There was intrigue at the Vadolcadium, possibly more. It seems I cannot escape it."

"You're right. Where there's power, there's intrigue. I did have a difficult time at first, that's true. But much of that was my own attitude. Once I came to know the people, I grew to love it here. But never once did I miss the intrigues of the palace. Life here was simpler but deeper, if you understand me."

"I believe I do." Falken raised his glass again. Two things he liked to indulge when he'd had a healthy amount of wine: conversation and toasts. "To backwaters filled with...water, and to places free of intrigue."

"Hear, hear," Domlen said, appearing amused.

They gently clinked their glasses together. After the toast, they sat in easy silence for a time. He wished the stars were visible. Then again, this little area Domlen had set up was far better than what had waited here the last time he'd been on the top of the tower. He didn't have to think hard to remember it. Soaked by the rain, his magic taken from him, about to be sacrificed so his blood would fuel a curse-breaker spell. Now he stretched out his legs toward the heat in the fire pit, feeling the soles of his boots warm through, making his toes warm. He had to admit, part of him was more than a little touched Domlen had gone through all this... But for what end?

The obvious answer would be that Lord Domlen Jadale wanted something. If they had been at court, that would've been the first thing to suspect. Patronage, support for some scheme, an ally before the king, any number of possibilities. Falken had seen and heard them all. But Domlen only seemed to want to end this curse. So far, everything he'd done had been to that end. So where did this fit into it? The answer was simple. It didn't. Domlen had his chance to kill him and complete the spell…and hadn't. For that choice, he'd suffered the backlash of the energy he'd stirred to life. No small thing, either. Falken had heard of sorcerers being killed by far smaller mistakes. If he no longer wanted Falken's blood for the ritual, then perhaps this was to ensure that when Falken left, he kept his pledge and sought the help of the grandmaster of the Vadolcadium to break this curse and free the spirits.

Unless… He paused, struck by the sudden thought. Unless Domlen was simply lonely.

He glanced at the large man who was sitting in his chair, leaning toward the fire pit with a glass in one hand and the other held toward the flames for warmth. The firelight glow tinted his face in reds and oranges like a sunset.

"We're not that different," Falken said gently, almost as if he spoke to himself as he turned to stare into the flames. "Neither of us have any love for the scheming and machinations of the royal court. We both have responsibilities, burdens most others don't understand." He sighed softly. "At times in our lives, we both have been surrounded by people who don't value us for who we are."

Domlen set his glass aside, stood, and moved closer to the fire. He stood there, a big man casting a big shadow. The smoke poured from the flap near the top of the fire, but the rain dripping in fell in a puddle way from the coals and logs. He set another log on the flames. Sparks drifted upward.

"You're right," he finally said, still facing the fire. "But to me, those things no longer matter very much. Now I only have one thing that matters."

Falken didn't have to ask what that was, and Domlen left

it unsaid. The curse on the fortress, the curse on his people. He regretted making the comparison between them only a moment ago. If their situations were reversed, could he have been as strong? Could he have stayed here alone in a stronghold full of ghosts who once were people he'd known and loved, all the while understanding that one day they would destroy him unless he found some way to break a curse so powerful even the Boa Visk had fled it? He couldn't answer, for he didn't know. And what did he truly comprehend of this man's lonely existence here in a land empty of everything? He whined that his cruel brothers did not love him and how his father was a coldhearted and scheming bastard, but what was that compared to the things Domlen had endured?

He stood and went to him. He put his hand on the man's back, feeling the heavy muscles there, just beneath his tunic. All he wanted was some way to make things right for once. That was one of the things he hated most about being the third son with the least power: it was far from easy to fix the things his kin ruined.

Domlen turned to face him. The firelight made his rough-hewn features seem almost magical, those shifting orange and yellow glows mixed with the shadows and turned him even more striking than usual. They stood there, neither speaking, looking into each other's eyes, the air around them heavy with a growing tension, an expectation…

When Domlen leaned down and captured his lips in a kiss, it was no surprise to Falken. The moment had felt exactly right for just such a kiss. So he closed his eyes, gave himself to the kiss, yielded to the other man's lips as the kiss grew fiercer. Domlen's arms came up around him. Falken made a little groan of pleasure when those strong arms held him tighter. His skin felt flushed, and his heart pounded harder. His cock stirred to life, desperate for attention after all this time. He suspected Domlen could feel it, because he gave a growl and pulled Falken even tighter to him.

The kiss was perfect, save that it did not last forever.

All at once, Domlen stepped away from him, his eyes wide, emotions flitting across his face so quickly that Falken had trouble reading them, especially on a man who was usually so implacably controlled. Domlen lifted his hands, whether to draw Falken closer again or push him away, he wasn't certain. Then he let his hands fall back to his sides. There was such a look of pain and doubt on his face that it tore at Falken's heart.

He looked up into Domlen's face, unwilling to look away, unwilling to ignore what had happened. He didn't know how he would feel about the kiss tomorrow, but right now it had grown perfectly from the moment. He prayed that Domlen did not regret it, but from his reaction, he clearly did.

"What is wrong?" Falken asked softly. His voice was soft, here, when in his past life—the one he'd lived as a prince in Teirlan—he would've demanded.

"I shouldn't have done that," Domlen replied, his expression darkening.

"What do you mean? It was a kiss, not a blow."

"I have no right to kiss a man I imprisoned." He took another step away, shaking his head rapidly back and forth. "I have no right to kiss a man I nearly murdered. You said as much yourself."

Falken watched him, his heart aching, but he didn't know how to reassure the man. The guilt in his eyes was drowning him. But how could he convince him that this was right? That there was something between them they should not ignore.

Domlen would not believe his words. And yet, he had to try.

"Don't ruin the kiss for me," he said. "I enjoyed it. Gods, I more than enjoyed it. And I am more than capable of looking out for myself now."

But Domlen turned away, broad shoulders hunched, his fists clenched, his head down.

"Tell me," Falken said, wanting to touch him, to reassure him, but uncertain how it would be taken. Would it bring him closer or push him farther away? "What is eating at you? Tell me what is wrong."

"You will go home. I will stay here."

"I go seeking answers. When I have the knowledge we need, I will return." He looked the other man straight in the eye, willing him to believe. "I vow that I will return."

But Domlen shook his head. "I must stand vigil here. I know the knife can...destroy the spirits if they become revenir. If we can't save them...I will do what needs to be done."

Falken reached out and grabbed the other man's hand, holding it tight. "We will save them, Domlen. That is a promise."

"I cannot fail them again. After I do what must be done, I would have no reason to live. I won't stay here and rot, lord of a fortress so empty it no longer has ghosts. Only rain."

"Come to Teirlan then. With me."

The words jumped out of his mouth, but after he said them, he knew he meant them, even as he realized it was impossible. His father would never trust Domlen, and his brothers would be even less inclined to give their trust. Falken could tell them that Domlen Jadale had the ancient blood of kings in his bloodline, but only his current fortunes would matter at court. The Jadales were a diminished line. As unfair as that might be, it was the truth.

"My duty is to Tharsgald," Domlen said, the emotion in his words so tightly bound it seemed as if those words must burst apart. "My duty is here."

"Not if the fortress is empty. There's nothing to defend."

Domlen swept a hand at the empty plates and the mostly empty bottles of wine. "This was a parting feast for you, Prince Falken. The best of what little I still have. When you are strong enough, on the morrow, or the next day, take the rest of my gold and the horse and make your way home with my blessings."

Falken reached for him, but Domlen drew away. The prince wasn't willing to let it end like that. Not with his lips still tingling from their kiss. Not with this ache inside him. One that warmed his heart, yet made him deeply afraid it was all in vain.

"I mean what I say, Domlen." He drew himself up, chin high, shoulders back. "I will find an answer and I will return. Wait for me. Please."

Domlen smiled, but it was full of sorrow. He turned his head away to stare off beyond the battlements at the dark clouds, the jagged mountain peaks, and the ever-present rain.

CHAPTER TEN

Their kiss had been like sunshine breaking through the clouds. It had been life. It had been warmth. Passion. Connection. All things Domlen realized he wanted, things he deeply missed. Things he did not deserve.

He stood at the breach in the walls in the gray gloom of dawn, between the jagged edges of broken stone a full twelve paces across. Blasted open by Boa Visk sorcerers when the storm had stolen the power of the protective spells. He remembered standing here after the blast, with smoke all around him, his armor bloodstained, his sword blade bloodstained. He stood here and screamed a battle cry of defiance. Then the Boa Visk legion had stormed through the breach like an ocean wave. The bloodshed that had followed...the loss, the sorrow. He stood there now, rain pelting him, the water running over the tops of his boots, watching as the small branching streams came together and poured into the moat. From the moat, the water channeled into the river. From there to the ocean, leagues distant. He wished he could float away on that flow of water, but he knew it was cold, and he would die long before he reached the sand and the sun.

Prince Falken was a good man. He no longer doubted that the prince would return as promised after bringing the problem to the sorcerers in Lindermain. They, in time, might even be able to unravel what dark magic sustained this nightmare curse. Yet that was the problem. There wasn't enough time.

It had been four days since the kiss. The prince had not yet departed. He spent nearly all his hours in the library with Yosel, searching through the ancient texts and scrolls with a single-minded determination that Domlen couldn't help but admire. It touched his heart to see a man who had not started as a friend show such dedication to the plight of his people. Domlen did what he could to aid him, which wasn't much, and his uselessness frustrated him deeply.

Neither of them spoke of the kiss. The tension between them was stronger than it had been since the prince had been hurt by the revenir…by Pilla. He wanted to talk about it—a thousand times, he nearly said something. But fear always stopped him. He was a coward. Afraid of his feelings. Afraid of the prince leaving. Terrified he was unworthy. Uncertain of what the kiss could mean to them both. Was it simply the momentary passion of two men who had not had any pleasure for so long? Or was it something deeper? He didn't know. He didn't dare ask.

This was the eve of the blood moon. He knew and kept silent. He was uncertain whether the prince knew. Here was another chance to end this nightmare. Yet, not a chance at all, for he would not harm the prince. He could not harm him, no matter what it cost. Was that selfish? Cowardly? Was it right? He didn't know and could not say. All he knew was that it twisted his heart until it bled droplets of his soul.

The ghosts — *his* ghosts, his people — had grown stranger as the time of the blood moon approached. While this had always happened to some extent, now the effect seemed far more pronounced. He noticed more of the guards staring up into the sky at the storm clouds. Servants standing by themselves, unmoving, either silent or quietly murmuring broken sentences, their gazes far away. Even Yosel, the one spirit who had always seemed the most self-aware and vibrant, had grown slower to respond, more distant.

This was yet another thing he and Falken did not speak of, though they both knew it well. He could feel the weight of it crushing down on them. Domlen carried the dagger with him wherever he went, while Falken pored over the texts like a man possessed. He suspected it was the reason Falken had not yet departed. The prince must have realized there wasn't enough time to reach Teirlan, convince the sorcerers there to help, and return with a solution before the things they both feared came to pass. Revenir loosed into the countryside, beyond the rain-ravaged lands of the curse, to attack unsuspecting farmers and towns. All their hopes were pinned upon Falken discovering something inside the fortress's ancient books.

His heart had not been this full of doubt and despair since setting out on his journey to find a way to break the curse. Back then, he'd been determined. He'd told himself he only needed to find the answer and make it happen. His hand moved to his side where the dagger rested in its sheath. He touched the handle, disliking the feel of the smooth, polished bone. Once, he'd told himself he was willing to do whatever it took to save his people. Now he knew that was a lie. He wasn't strong enough, not cold enough. Now he feared he would have to do whatever it took to stop them.

Something touched his shoulder and he flinched. He wheeled around, his heart skipping a beat. He hadn't heard anyone approaching through the rain.

It was Ronev the guardsman. The man Pilla had intended to marry. He drew back a little from Domlen's startled reaction, though his movements were slower than usual.

"My lord," Ronev said, concern on his young face. "It is not good to stand out here in this downpour. You will catch your death."

Domlen stared at him. At first, Ronev's words did not register. Then Domlen gave a harsh and bitter laugh, while Ronev eyed him warily.

"Thank you for your concern, but I am fine. Merely reviewing the state of our defenses."

Ronev glanced at the gap in the fortifications. His face went through a series of expressions—surprise, confusion, alarm—as he looked at the blasted hole. The breach itself was one of those things the ghosts kept forgetting about because it hadn't existed until shortly before their deaths. The Boa Visk, however, they remembered well.

"We must fill that break in the wall," Ronev said. "I will alert the captain. We must station more men here to defend it."

Domlen tried his best to give the man an encouraging smile. "Good thinking, Ronev. See to it."

Ronev turned to go…then hesitated. He glanced back at Domlen, his eyes tinged with worry and giving off that slight ghostly glow. "My lord, have you seen Pilla? I cannot find her. I feel as though I've searched and searched. Where could she be?" He cast a fearful glance at the breach in the walls. "You do not think she's wandered away, out of the fortress?" He started for the gap. "I must go to her."

"She has not gone beyond the walls," Domlen assured him again, his heart breaking a piece at a time. "You have my word, Ronev. I have been watching."

Ronev stopped, though he seemed deeply torn. The worry in his expression deepened. "Perhaps she's gotten lost in the cellars or...fallen into the cistern." He hesitated again. "I've often felt strange of late, my lord." He glanced at the sky. "I keep thinking about the red moon. And somehow, I'm certain it has something to do with Pilla. Yet, it is as if I'm dreaming..."

"Dreams are dreams." Domlen nodded toward the fortress keep and felt the lie try and lodge in his throat. "Go. Tell the captain of the breach and then continue your search for your love. I know you will find her."

Ronev saluted and trotted back to the keep. Domlen watched him go, every part of him cold and aching and tired. He turned away from the sight, but his legs felt weak, his body that of an old man. He fell to his knees, then forward, catching himself on his outthrust hands. Jolts of pain shot through his forearms and knees as they impacted the courtyard flagstones. Cold rainwater runoff flowed over his hands, soaked through his breeches at the knees and down his shins. It numbed him. He stared at his hands beneath the flow of water, pale and distorted.

This had to end. He only wished he knew how to end it without losing everything. When he wept, the tears mixed with the rain and hid them.

Then warm arms suddenly enfolded him. A voice he

knew began speaking in his ear, chiding him, the concern in the tone readily apparent. Prince Falken helped him back to his feet. The hood of his cloak was pushed back. The rain had soaked his hair and plastered it to his head. Falken moved to his side and pressed against him. He put his arm around Domlen's waist and hooked Domlen's arm around his shoulders.

"Let's get you inside," the prince said. "Get you warm."

Together they slowly made their way back into the keep, to his chambers, where there was fire in the hearth, and heat and light.

* * *

Falken didn't allow his mind to fill with thoughts as he guided Domlen to a spot near the hearth inside his chambers. The fire had burned low, so he busied himself stoking it back to life until it was bright and roaring again. He refused to allow himself to think because he was afraid of what those thoughts might be. He could sense the fear and worry inside his head, running in circles, gnawing desperately at his mind, and he could not give in to it.

Domlen stood behind him. His clothing was soaked. Water dripped from the edges onto the floor. When he lifted his hands toward the heat, Falken noticed he was still shivering. He'd first noticed Domlen shivering when he'd been body-to-body with him, helping support the man back to the keep, but he'd kept his mouth shut, his worry tied down tight like a ship prepared for a storm.

He stood from tending the fire, shrugged out of his wet

cloak, and hung it on a peg a little ways from the hearth. Then he went to Domlen and helped him remove his cloak. Domlen moved slowly, helping, but seeming as if his mind was not fully engaged in the task.

Gently, patiently, he began to undo the laces of Domlen's jerkin and then his doublet. Domlen's gaze met his, but the man did not otherwise react. He did not help with this, but neither he did he hinder. Falken eased the wet clothing off him and likewise hung them to dry.

He paused when he turned back to the man, drawing in a short breath at the impressive sight of him. Domlen was large, his chest broad and well-muscled, his arms thick, his shoulders like granite slabs. The firelight on his face and his bare skin made him seem almost dreamlike, a vision of male beauty in spite of his rough-hewn features...or perhaps because of them.

Falken had to stop himself from reaching for the other man. With a silent curse, he had to push away the stirrings of desire growing inside him. This was not the time for those feelings.

Domlen moved closer to the fire, staring down into the coals. His shivers diminished, which took the immediate edge off Falken's worry.

"Ronev spoke to me," Domlen said, surprising him.

His eyes narrowed as he watched the other man, but Domlen's face could have been a stone mountainside for all it told him. "Pilla's lover?"

Domlen nodded, still staring into the flames, his hands out to bask in the warmth. "He wanted me to come in from the rain." A smile crossed his lips and then vanished as if it had never existed. "Then he asked me about Pilla. I lied to him."

Falken wanted to go to him, to pull him into his arms and comfort him, help him release the pain inside him. But he didn't. He couldn't help but remember their last kiss. A kiss he had loved, but one that had stirred Domlen's guilt. In the end, the kiss seemed to drive them farther apart rather than draw them closer together.

Domlen suddenly lurched forward and slammed his fist into the stone mantelpiece over the hearth. It surprised Falken enough that he stepped backward with a cry. Domlen drew back his fist and hammered the mantle again, his face a mask of pain and fury.

"Stop that!" Falken said, grabbing his arm before he could strike again. "Don't do this to yourself."

Domlen wheeled to face him. Tears ran from his eyes, down his cheeks. His gaze burned as hot as the coals. "Why didn't you kill me?" The pain in his words was deeper than a stab wound. His next words came out on a furious sob. "Why would you show mercy? Damn you!" He wrenched free of Falken's hold, spun back to the hearth, and slammed his fist into the stone again. "Damn you. *Why?*" He hammered the mantelpiece over and over, his knuckles split and bleeding, leaving red smears on the gray stone.

Falken went to him and grabbed the man's arm at the elbow before he could deliver another blow. This time, Falken's grip stilled his punches, but the man was as rigid as ice. He trembled as he stared at the blood his split knuckles had left on the stone.

Falken's heart was pounding hard as he pulled the man into an embrace. At first, Domlen stayed as tense, as rigid and unmovable as the stone he'd attacked. Falken refused to let him go. He hugged him tighter, willing the other man to yield, to give in and embrace him back.

Domlen whispered repeated words, so faint that Falken barely caught them, and only because he held the man in his arms. "I cannot be forgiven… I cannot be forgiven."

What use were words and spoken reassurances here? How could they help against pain so deep it was like a wound that split a man in two? Domlen's hurt pierced all the way to his core. It had become a part of him that he could not escape. Falken knew he had to convince the lord of the fortress another way. Show him the truth with actions, not easy words. So even when Domlen started to draw away from him again, to close himself off and become the emotionless statue he'd been in the past, Falken refused to let him go. He used all his strength to hold the man so tightly he could feel the thump of Domlen's heart beating.

"I forgive you," Falken said quietly, holding him hard. "I forgive you, Domlen Jadale."

It was as if a mountain crumbled around him as Domlen's body finally gave in to the embrace. His big arms came up around Falken, clutching him tight. They stood there, not speaking, holding one another.

It was then that Falken realized exactly what he wanted. If Domlen could not find the strength to take what he so clearly needed, so deeply desired, then it was up to him to make it happen. In life, in love, fortune favored the bold.

So Falken broke the embrace, reached up, and wiped away Domlen's tears. Then he looped his arms around the man's neck and drew him down into a long kiss. There was passion in that kiss, but also healing. Both need and giving. After a moment, Domlen began to kiss him back.

Reluctantly, Falken ended the kiss, drawing back enough to look the other man in the eyes. Domlen's gaze was clear, not hidden behind that cold armor he'd always protected

himself with, and that made Falken's heart soar with
happiness. He took the man's bruised and bleeding hand and
lifted it, kissing the few places that were not scraped and
swelling. Domlen winced slightly but didn't draw his hand
away. Then Falken gently pulled him toward the bedroom.

They both needed this. They both needed the warmth of
body heat, the feel of two hearts beating, to touch, to love, to
remember they were alive and to celebrate it. It was dark
within the bedchambers and dark beyond the leaded
windows. He let go of Domlen long enough to light a lamp
but kept the flame low. The other man was watching him,
standing near the bed clad only in his breeches and boots, his
chest still bare, the jagged scar shockingly stark in the dim
light. Falken stared at that wound. He'd almost lost the man
long before he'd ever found him.

The prince slowly undid the laces of his doublet and
shrugged out of it, letting it fall to the floor unheeded. He
steadied himself against the table as he reached down and
yanked off first one boot, then the other, again letting them
fall where they may. He didn't take his eyes from Domlen,
holding the other man's gaze as though his life depended
upon never looking away. Domlen mirrored him, pulling off
his boots and setting them aside, but neatly and by the foot of
the bed, which pulled a small smile from Falken.

Then he went to Domlen, teasing him with another kiss
that left both their lips scorching. His thoughts were a dizzy
tumble as he ran his hands across the man's bare chest,
reveling in the feel of the hard muscles of his chest, the ridges
of his abdomen, across the wound that had healed so poorly.
He lovingly traced his fingers through the dark patch of hair
below his navel, along the waist of his breeches, and lower,
smiling when he found the man's cock hard and ready

beneath the cloth. He intensified the kiss, slipping his tongue into the other man's mouth as he caressed Domlen's cock through his breeches until he got what he wanted from the man—a groan of pure pleasure. Then he brought his other hand up to trail a finger around Domlen's nipple, teasing that until it stood up hard and tight.

He broke the kiss to dip his head to that nipple, taking it in his mouth gently as the hard muscle of the man's pectorals twitched. He licked the nipple, nipped at it softly with his teeth until he again got what he desired: another moan. This moan was chased by Domlen's quick indrawn breath as Falken kissed lower, down the ridges of his abdominals. His fingers deftly worked the laces open, and then he slowly drew down the man's breeches until his cock sprang free, long and thrusting upward from his body.

He was rock hard himself as he went to his knees on the rug in front of the other man and took his cock, unable to completely encircle its impressive width with his forefinger and thumb before lowering his mouth to it.

Domlen whispered his name when he took that cock deep into his mouth, working his hand in the opposite direction. He kept up a steady rhythm, though at times he tormented the man by withdrawing Domlen's cock enough to run his tongue across the glans, along the tip to taste him, then plunging back down on it. It wasn't long until Domlen's hand was fisted in Falken's hair, his head thrown back as he lost himself in the pleasure. Falken loved that look, loved the power he had to make Domlen feel this way. It made him feel powerful, feel important and wanted. He could look at Domlen like this for the rest of his days and not count them wasted.

Finally, he felt Domlen's body tensing and the man

growled, "Too good. Your mouth…too good." His grip tightened in Falken's hair as he moved away to keep from losing control.

Understanding, Falken let him go with a wicked grin. Then he climbed back to his feet and skinned off his own breeches, letting his own erection free. Domlen pulled him into another kiss, capturing his mouth, pulling them tight against each other, cock to cock. He slowly began to grind against Falken's cock. Waves of pleasure traveled through his body as he mirrored the movement. He was aching for this man. He needed the touch, the warmth. And no one else's touch would do. This was healing; this was connection.

He turned to climb onto the bed, positioning himself for the other man. Domlen's hot gaze seared along his skin, burning with desire, his cock rock hard, weeping precum from its slit and still wet from Falken's mouth.

Domlen withdrew a small bottle from one of the table drawers, poured out a slippery oil, and coated his cock with it. Then he went to Falken and moved behind him. Falken closed his eyes and drew in a short breath as the other man's hands caressed his buttocks, then gently stroked his balls, before they returned to his back entrance. A moment later, he felt Falken's finger coating him with the oil, then pushing carefully inside him, preparing him.

A groan of need and pleasure escaped him when he felt Domlen's cock at his entrance, pressing slowly but irresistibly in. Then he was taking the other man into himself, being filled by him. He was rocked forward by Domlen's thrusts as they began slow and steady and grew faster as his pleasure increased. Falken braced himself, his eyes closed, breathing fast at the incredible feeling of being taken by this man. He lost himself in the pleasure, time becoming meaningless, until

Domlen's thrusts became fast and frantic and he felt the man come undone behind him.

He was just opening his eyes, feeling Domlen's cock pulsing within him, when Domlen slowly withdrew, then turned him over so that Falken lay on his back with his legs spread, his cock still rigid and aching for attention. Domlen gave it that attention, taking it in his mouth, leaning over him, and working his firm lips along his length. Falken buried his hand in the other man's hair, helplessly clutching him. Domlen worked his head up and down, faster, faster. Falken could no longer hold back and didn't try. He reached the cliff and tumbled over it, his entire body tensing as he shot his seed into the other man's mouth. Domlen didn't stop working him with his mouth, sucking him, milking him and swallowing until Falken was drained and done and every part of him was feeling warm and sated.

Only then did Domlen lie down on the bed beside him and draw Falken into his arms. They lay there together for a long time, feeling their hearts beating fast, listening to the crackle of fire from the hearth in the outer chamber.

"That was wonderful," Falken murmured, laying his head on the other man's chest, hearing the thump of his heart. "Perfect."

Domlen slowly stroked his back. After a pause, he said, "I am not worthy of you."

Falken glanced at him, frowning. "I am the one who decides who is worthy of me and who is not."

"You are a prince."

"I am the third son of a king who never wasted much love on any of his offspring. I am a sorcerer, useful and valuable to my father, but more outcast than cherished scion. And I shall say it again. *I determine who is worthy of me.*"

"I have nothing to offer you. This place was given to me to rule, by a king's decree, the pass to hold and the people to protect. I did neither. My blood is tainted." He looked down at his swollen hand. The blood from the scrapes on his knuckles had dried, but the damaged skin still looked raw and painful and bruised. "This...this was like a dream to me. A wonderful dream I wasn't worthy of."

Falken pushed himself to a sitting position. The hot surge of frustration and anger surprised him, but he hated hearing Domlen talking about himself in such a way. He had to make the man see he was valuable, he was an equal, how there was always cause for hope, and despair was not inevitable.

"This is no dream." He touched Domlen's chest, feeling the warmth grow where their skin met. "This is very real. Your blood is not tainted, no matter what they told you at court. Your ancestors were the same as mine, the blood of kings. So you are worthy. But that doesn't matter. We could've had this even were you some son a merchant or even a baseborn bastard. A prince chooses his lovers."

He expected Domlen to come back with a challenge, claiming how neither of them were truly free to choose their lovers, not with matters of heirs and statehood and family lines at hand.

Instead, Domlen watched him intently, his brows creased into a frown. "Where did you hear that? About my ancestors."

He hesitated, suddenly uneasy. He'd spoken without thinking, desperate to get Domlen to understand what he meant. It was simple. He hadn't wanted Domlen to build yet another wall between them.

"Yosel told me. He told me all about your arrival to take control of the fortress. Who you were and from where you hailed. He cares deeply for you and was happy to talk about you."

"You must be mistaken. He has never said that to me."

Falken shifted until he could kiss the man, which he did, softly and tenderly. "It doesn't matter. I only sought to stop you from keeping your distance from me, believing you were doing what was right."

Domlen was lying there beside him, slowly stroking his hand along Falken's back, a comforting touch. He didn't answer, but neither did he draw away.

Falken was drifting off to sleep when a horrible realization jerked him awake again, his heart pounding hard and fast. Domlen hadn't known he'd had the blood of ancient kings in his line. Yosel hadn't told him—Falken had known that much—but apparently either Domlen's mother and father were ignorant of the fact or, if his father intended to tell him when he was older, he'd died fighting wars in other lands before he could. It made sense of course. Like a fool, Falken had carelessly blurted it out because he'd wanted to stop Domlen from thinking himself unworthy to be with a prince.

He pushed himself up on one elbow so he could look Domlen in the eyes. "I will find a way to break the curse here. You must have faith in me. There is always another way."

Domlen met his gaze but did not answer right away. Then, softly, he said, "We are running out of time."

"I only need a little longer. I'm close, I know it. We'll set them free, Domlen. We both will do it."

Domlen nodded. Yet, even as Falken settled his head back on Domlen's chest, lying here together warm in his bed, he wondered what was going through the other man's mind. He couldn't shake his worry that his careless words had done more harm than good.

CHAPTER ELEVEN

It was barely dawn when Domlen disentangled himself from the sleeping prince and carefully climbed out of bed. He dressed quickly in dry clothes, started a fire in the hearth so Falken could wake to a warm room, and then he left. He made his way through the fortress to the library. It was disquieting, walking through the fortress. It was far more silent than usual. The servants and guards he saw were slow to bow but not due to any insolence. They didn't seem to realize he was there at first. When they did notice him, they seemed surprised, as if startled out of a daydream. By the time he reached the library, the hairs on the back of his arms and neck were standing up.

He'd brought the dagger along with him, though he prayed he wouldn't need it, that he was only being overly cautious. All the same, it was a comfort to have the blade at his side, though not a comfort he enjoyed.

Last night, he'd hardly slept. Finally, utter exhaustion had taken him. He still felt all brittle inside, full of broken pieces he was unsure would ever fit together again. Being with the prince had been a beautiful, wondrous thing. A time he would never forget. Yet as he'd lain there with Falken snoring softly in his arms, his mind had remained at war with itself.

After they made love, part of him had felt completed, content…happy. It had been a very long time since he'd felt at peace. But then he'd worried about whether he was worthy of the prince's affections after all he'd done, after everything he'd failed. When the prince revealed that Domlen had the blood of kings, he'd known at once what the implications were. Falken had realized it too. He'd seen it in the other man's eyes, but it had been too late to take the words back. It was why the prince had been so keen to reassure him that an answer could be found in the books. Perhaps an answer could be found here…perhaps not. But it was taking too long. The ghosts would change. From their behavior, it would be soon. Domlen would be forced to utterly destroy them…or they might destroy him and begin the rampage he feared. Either way, he wouldn't be freeing their spirits from the curse and opening their path to the afterlife. He would have failed.

But there was still a way to end it. All he needed was to speak with Yosel and hear the truth for himself. Then the path forward would be clear.

He felt calm as he entered the library. Soon he would know, and the very act of knowing would give him power. He would no longer be helpless. For too long he'd felt powerless, tossed about by the whims of cruel fate. The Boa Visk had captured him and thrown him into the fortress dungeons after making him watch the butchery of the fortress household and guard, but they'd refused to execute him and give him that one cold mercy. They'd intended him for something else, some other degradation, but their magic had gone berserk, the ghosts of the people they'd murdered returned and hunted them. The storm they'd raised would not end, flooding the land and ruining the crops while he rotted helpless in the cell. Even after the Boa Visk fled and he was freed, he'd been unable to help the spirits of his people enter the afterworld. The countryside quickly emptied of people fleeing the Boa Visk and the floods, meaning he had failed to protect them as well.

True, he'd reclaimed some of his initiative when he'd set out on his journey for answers and then later, when he'd abducted the prince and smuggled him back to the fortress. But ever since he'd dropped the knife instead of using it to complete the ritual, he'd felt increasingly ineffectual. He couldn't help Falken with his research because he didn't speak the language of the oldest, most valuable books. He could no longer risk another journey now that the spirits of the fortress were acting so odd, and now that they'd lost Pilla, driving deep that spike of his failure. He was trapped here, unable to act.

But now, he had a path and a plan.

The library was murky with shadow. The world outside the large windows was dreary, with wind blowing the rain against the leaded glass so hard it sounded as if pebbles were being thrown. Tonight was the blood moon. He wondered if there would be a rage storm to accompany it and decided it didn't matter.

Yosel was seated at one of the long tables. A stack of books sat before him, but he was only sitting there unmoving while staring at the bookshelves opposite him.

A chill went up Domlen's spine. No, please. Not Yosel…

"It is dark in here," Domlen said carefully, praying the old sage would respond to his words and not be like Pilla before she turned into the revenir. "Why are there no candles? And the hearth is cold."

The old man turned to look his way. He didn't appear any older than he ever had since returning as a spirit...but Domlen had the feeling the man had aged somehow, grown wearier.

"I am no longer cold," Yosel said in a flat voice. "Isn't that a curious thing?"

Domlen walked closer to him, feeling the weight of the blade in the sheath at his hip. His heard was thudding; his mouth was dry as sand. "Are you well, Yosel?"

"No, I am not well. I've decided I am tired. I am ready to move on."

"So you know." It wasn't the first time Yosel had realized he was a spirit, neither would it be the last. The old sage had a brilliant mind, though even his considerable mental powers were sometimes muddled and confused about what was real in this true world where he was trapped as a spirit.

"I know something is deeply wrong. With everything here. Your young friend has been here for all hours of the daylight with you. It helps me...keep recent memories in my mind." He reached out a thin, spotted hand to Domlen. Domlen moved closer and took it. The old man's skin felt very cold to the touch. It also seemed to vibrate a little.

Yosel smiled. "A blind man would've figured it out sooner than I. Your skin is so warm, and I am so cold. I dismissed it as my age, the furnace inside me slowly going out, but that was wrong. Something terrible happened here..."

"The Boa Visk attacked us. They started a storm that

depleted the power of the spells in the walls. They blasted their way inside and killed all within. Including you."

"Ah, that is not a happy story," Yosel said, frowning and staring up at the shadow-shrouded ceiling beams. "Storms have a will of their own, thus it is no wonder they had trouble controlling it. Perhaps...hmm." He waved his hand as if dismissing the thought. "Never mind me. Simply speculating." He glanced at Domlen and gave him a tired smile. "So how might I help you, lord?"

"Do I have the blood of royalty in my veins?"

Yosel gave a grim chuckle as Domlen waited patiently for him to answer. "Direct and to the point as always, aren't you? The answer is yes. The Jadale family line can be traced all the way back to the Jadale kings, men who held power before the Teirlan invasion that brought them down, hundreds and hundreds of years ago. Your ancestors were marginalized, though they still had wealth and power and noble titles. Over time, the wealth and power faded. One of your ancestors, Grivton Jadale, attempted to overthrow the crown and restore the dynasty. He was killed, and the Jadales fell farther, banned from mentioning their history under threat of attainder. That was well over a hundred years past, but the distrust persists." He sighed and patted Domlen on the hand. "In the beginning, when you were given this fortress to rule in the name of King Leovic, I was ordered by certain retainers at the court to keep an eye on you. Watch for rebellious inclinations." He chuckled again and shook his head.

"Why didn't you ever tell me?"

"Perhaps I should have. But I still believe that if you didn't know, and your parents did not tell you, then perhaps that was for the best. Your ancestors had trouble forgetting their royal past, much to their sorrow. If you were content being the son of a general loyal to the crown, then stirring up long ago histories and wrongs would benefit none of us."

"You told Prince Falken."

That earned him a grin and a wink from the old man. It seemed the longer Yosel talked, the more animated he became. Domlen wondered if that might be a way to help stop the ghosts from losing their essential selves...or at least slow the process.

"Did I?" Yosel asked. "My apologies, I'm sure I likely did, but the specifics are hazy. Although the young prince *is* very curious about you, I have noticed. That, and I've always liked to ramble. He seems a good man, though."

"He is that." Domlen stood. "Thank you for telling me the truth. It has helped me more than you know."

The old sage beamed at him. "Glad to hear, glad to hear. If you ever need anything, please don't be shy. Now, I think I'll just sit here and let my mind drift a little. Until that polite young prince comes by, asking for so many different and very ancient books. So exciting for an old scholar..."

Domlen left him sitting in the gloom, staring at the bookshelves as the rain tapped at the window as if wanting to be let inside.

He knew what he had to do now. He only prayed that Prince Falken could find it in his heart to forgive him one more time.

CHAPTER TWELVE

The winds began picking up in the evening. A particularly strong gust rattled the windowpanes in the library where Falken had been working since shortly after he'd woken alone in Domlen's bed. He was hunched over a volume with cracked leather bindings, trying not to damage the pages as he turned them with the utmost care. He hadn't seen Domlen since they'd shared their midmorning meal together. Domlen had surprised him. Falken had been afraid the man might withdraw into himself or have regrets after the night they'd shared together, especially after Falken had seen him so vulnerable. He had finally seen beneath Domlen's armor. But Domlen had been attentive and warm. Gods, the man had even smiled more than once during the meal. If some heavy lovemaking was all it took to make the man open up, Falken only regretted waiting this long.

But then Falken had left to continue his research at the

library, while Domlen had said he wanted to check on the spirits, which had been acting strangely of late. Soon enough Falken had thrown himself into his search and lost track of time. Now the sun had dropped below the horizon beyond the mountains and the low storm cover, and he was startled to realize how dark it had become.

He sighed and pushed back from the book he'd been studying. It was a tome on healing critical wounds to the body in the moments before a spirit could cross into the afterlife. An invaluable text, but not what he was searching for, though at first he'd believed it might help release the spirits trapped here. He was having trouble concentrating. He knew the reaction between two opposing magics had created the curse, which were actually side effects of an out-of-control spell. But the solartia spells were useless without the sunlight, and he knew little about Boa Visk sorceries. The same energy feeding the storm had trapped the ghosts. But how to stop that loop?

He cursed and shut the book again. Yosel was sitting in a chair by himself, but at the sound of the book closing, he turned toward Falken. Then he smiled and wandered over to him.

"Not going well?" he asked gently.

"No. Not going well."

"Perhaps we are not thinking along the path we need to think," Yosel said.

Falken's mouth tightened. "I would say that is abundantly clear...but doesn't help me much. I need to stop magic created and designed to never stop."

"No small task. But perhaps if we think of the specific pieces it will help. If the power is moving through a door or drawn here through an opening in the veil to feed the magic, then perhaps we shouldn't consider unmaking the spell, but starving it. What if there was a simple way to jam the door shut? Perhaps with something anti-magical..."

The crovmane bracers. Of course.

Falken sat there, completely stunned. He was a damned fool not to have thought of it right away. He knew that the mystical energy constantly feeding the storm had trapped the spirits on this plane of existence, keeping the pathways to the afterlife closed to them. He'd been trying to discover how to unmake the curse, end the storm, and free the spirits—the *results* of the events set in motion by an initial catastrophe. But what if he could close down the power source itself? Not cancelling the Boa Visk magic, but damming the flow of power. Best of all, it wouldn't require the devastating power and high costs of the spell the warlock had given Domlen. Even a minor disruption might throw the entire looping channel out of true enough to let it naturally decay with time. It wouldn't be easy, especially without the laboratories of the Vadolcadium, but with the crovmane bracers, he had the core of what he would need.

He stood, wanting to share the insight with Domlen. To Yosel, he said, "You are brilliant. Domlen is lucky to have you."

"Ah, Domlen..." The old man's smile gradually turned into a frown. "He was here...earlier today...I think. Asking..."

Falken froze. He tried to keep his voice carefully neutral. "Asking about what?"

"He asked about his bloodline," Yosel replied. "An odd thing for him to ask, as he never had brought it up before..."

Icy fear ran straight through Falken as he stood there unable to reply. His legs felt weak. His blood was rushing in his ears. He quickly did a calculation in his mind. Tonight might very well be another blood moon.

No. His fears had to be wrong. Domlen couldn't be considering another ritual, this time using himself and his blood as the fuel to power the breaking spell. He wouldn't do that, not after what they'd just experienced together. Not after Falken had promised to find a way.

He stood there, thoughts racing through his head, wanting to run to Domlen, but his body not responding. He felt fear, most of it was fear, but there was also hurt. Hurt that Domlen didn't have enough faith to wait for him to find a solution that didn't end a tragedy with yet another tragedy.

But he had also come to know the man. And if Domlen believed he was doing the right thing for his people, he would do so, no matter the cost to himself.

Falken looked out the window again as his heart picked up speed and his breath came faster. Darkness. Rain. But the moon would be over the horizon. He had no idea how much time he had left. If Domlen intended anything mad, he would have to do it from atop the tower where the focus circle was carved into the stone.

Falken finally got himself moving again. Once he took a step and broke the paralysis holding him, it was easy to run. Yosel called out to him, but he didn't stop. All he could think of was Domlen and the chance he would do something incredibly reckless and stupid and costly. The fool. The damned noble fool. He believed he had to take all of this onto himself. But they had so much to live for together, and now with Falken's discovery there was clear hope, not simply words and reassurances.

The halls and doors to other rooms flashed by as he ran for the main entrance to the central keep. Once, he skidded on a rug and went sprawling with a surprised curse. He scrambled back to his feet and ran onward. The darkness in the fortress was thick. He wished he'd brought one of the lamps along, although he probably would've broken it when he slipped—

He nearly fell again when the revenir floated out of the wall and headed straight for him. At one time, the revenir had been a guardsman, although Falken could only the man's tabard and mail, he'd changed so much as to be unrecognizable. The revenir made an eager hissing sound, his eyes burning red.

With a cry, he slid to a stop and began to run the other way. The revenir followed, drifting through the air, the toes of his boots floating a full handbreadth above the tiles. The revenir wasn't faster than he was, but he doubted it would ever tire. He dashed through hallways, circling around the keep, searching for another exit. Soon he had left the revenir behind, although he was gasping for air and had a stitch in his side.

He made it all the way back to the main doors when the revenir appeared again, floating through a solid oak door farther down another hallway. Falken turned on it, panting hard, and used his magic to open a crystal barrier of light in front of it. The revenir hit the barrier and rebounded, unable to pass through. The hungry phantom floated back and forth, searching for a way past, its red eyes blazing and never leaving Falken.

The prince turned and threw open the heavy double doors, running out into the darkness and rain. The stone was slick and treacherous, slowing him. A hissing scream sounded behind him. He glanced behind to see the revenir giving chase, having discovered a way around his barrier.

He ran faster, reckless and desperate now. He reached the tower. He meant to shove the tower door inward, but it was locked and barred, so he only hit it hard with his shoulder and rebounded, falling to the wet flagstones. With a curse, he seized his magic and pushed himself back to his feet. The revenir was still behind him but closing in.

He worked his will upon the primal forces and reached out and touched the locked door in the center. He spoke one word in High Urrian. Cracks opened up in the heavy wood, spreading out in zigzags from the middle, where his finger had pressed. Splinters flew as the cracks spread wider. Then the door simply fell apart.

Lightning flashed three times in rapid succession over the dark shapes of the mountains. It lit up the entire courtyard. He looked behind him again. The revenir had closed within a dozen paces and watched him eagerly.

He wasted no more time. He ran up the steps, pushing himself hard. By the time he reached the top landing, he was gasping for breath, the pain in his side became a knife stab, and the muscles in his thighs were burning. A glance at the steps leading to the tower roof told him all he needed to know. Drips of water trailed up the steps. That was where Domlen had gone.

Just as he'd feared.

Panic took hold of him. He ran up the stairs and crashed against the door. This door was not locked. It swung open easily, spilling him onto the roof in a clumsy tumble.

Domlen was on his knees in the focus circle. The altar was already prepared in the center. He held the dagger with the green blade in his hand. He was chanting. His eyes were closed. With the wind and the thunder, Falken realized Domlen had not heard him burst out of the door.

The air was charged with mystical energy, raw and powerful. More lightning flashed across the sky. The wind at the top of the tower was far worse than down in the courtyard. It pushed at him as if trying to throw him over the battlements to the flagstones far below.

"Domlen, no!" he screamed, lurching back to his feet and sucking in great gasps of air. He couldn't seem to catch his breath. He felt weak and unsteady from his nightmare run up the tower stairs. "This isn't the way!"

Domlen's eyes flew open. Emotions flashed across his face. Had Falken once believed the man as emotionless as a statue? Now it seemed as though he could read every thought there, every fear. Guilt, determination, sorrow, fear, and love. Yes, the warmth of love when he looked back into Falken's eyes. But that didn't stop him from raising the blade into the air, holding the knife in both hands and pointing downward, meaning to drive it into his stomach.

"No!" He started to run for Domlen, but then the revenir floated over the side of the tower as if scaling such a huge structure had been no more taxing than drifting in a strong current. He'd known the revenir would follow, but he'd expected it to chase him up the stairs. Not float upward in a direct line from the courtyard to the tower top, cutting his head start down to almost nothing.

Now the revenir was between them, cutting Falken off. Its eyes flashed a deeper red and it moved on him. He staggered back a step, terror seizing him. The revenir raised spindly arms to seize him.

"Falken!" Domlen yelled, raw panic in his voice. He pushed himself off his knees and turned the knife toward the revenir.

But the revenir seized Falken before he could move. Its

touch was shockingly cold and jerked a pained gasp from his lips. It lifted him effortlessly, but instead of immediately feeding, it carried him as it drifted toward the edge of the battlements.

The revenir meant to take him over the side, away from Domlen and the blade. Even if Domlen came after it with the knife, he wouldn't reach it in time. The revenir would float back to the ground with Falken clutched in its ice-cold arms and begin to drain the life out of him.

He struggled, trying to break free, but it was useless. He could see Domlen staring at him, pale, horror-stricken. Then Domlen raised the dagger started his chant again. The revenir had almost reached the crenels, meaning to float over the top and bring Falken into the cold air empty of everything but rain.

Domlen drove the dagger into his abdomen, shoving it beneath the rib cage to pierce his heart. A wordless wail escaped Falken's lips as he watched the life flee Domlen's eyes. The man he loved slumped to the stone, blood mixing with the rainwater.

The blast wave of mystic energy, released as the powerful spell was completed, hit Falken like a kick, driving all the breath out of him. The flare of red light was blinding as it shot into the sky, piercing the clouds, flooding the fortress walls. The wind stopped all at once. The rain vanished.

The revenir screamed and thrashed and changed as the energy enveloped it. It dropped Falken right at the edge of the battlements. He fell to the stones, landing on the tower roof instead of tumbling to his death. The blast wave hurled it into the night sky. Its features shifted, distorted, changed back to those of a young guardsman. Not Ronev but someone else. Domlen would know his name, he thought, as the ghost seemed to come apart like smoke.

He sobbed as his head cleared and he realized what Domlen had done to save him from the revenir. No. No. *NO!*

He scrambled and skidded along the wet stones until he reached Domlen's side. Blood was pouring from the deep wound. The dagger was lying in a puddle. The rain was slowly washing the blade clean again. Falken sobbed freely, shaking so badly he could hardly hold onto Domlen, his sorrow was so vast it threatened to crush him to nothing.

Text in High Urrian burst into his mind like lightning strike. The book on healing he had been reading earlier today, of course! But there wasn't much time — he had to act now.

He quickly set both hands on Domlen's open wound and summoned his power, calling to mind all the information he had gleaned. He spoke the words in High Urrian as he willed what he wished to happen, calling the mystic energy to his bidding. He healed and he burned, stopping the blood flow, cauterizing the wound. But even with the wound closed, Domlen had already died, and his heart had stopped. He needed more power!

Wild desperation seized him. He kept one hand on Domlen's chest, over his heart, the other he lifted to the sky and he willed and channeled power from those dark clouds even as they were beginning to disperse. The storm was ending. His time was running out. But he only used the last of his strength in one final, desperate summoning...

A lightning bolt shot down and hit his hand, striking the place where he'd forged his connection with the power in the sky. He served as a conduit for the power, directing it into Domlen, restarting his heart as the text had claimed was possible, while the rest of the power he desperately shunted off into the stone around him. Every muscle in his body went rigid. He nearly bit off the tip of his tongue when his jaws clacked shut hard. The pain was so great that it was too big to grasp.

He was knocked sprawling, thrown from Domlen to crumple to the wet stones. He tried to move, but his body wouldn't respond. The best he could do was blink tears out of his eyes. Tears only, because the rain had stopped. Overhead, he could see stars as the clouds dissipated.

Suddenly his view of the stars was blocked as Domlen bent over him. His onetime captor was very pale, looking extremely exhausted, but from his body heat, Falken knew he was alive. Alive and not a ghost. Alive and warm and *living* and that was all that mattered.

"You saved me," Domlen was telling him, kissing him, holding him.

Falken smiled. He wanted to kiss the man back, but he didn't have an ounce of strength. He felt as though a giant had picked up his body and wrung him out like a wet cloth until he had nothing left. "Look," was all he could whisper, glancing up at the sky.

Domlen looked up at the sky and shared the joy with him.

The rain had stopped. The clouds were gone. The stars shone overhead, and they were beautiful.

EPILOGUE

Prince Falken woke to a room full of brilliant sunlight. He blinked slowly at the brightness, trying to get his eyes to adjust. He turned his head, squinting at the windows. They were open. A warm breeze was blowing in. But the thing he noticed most was the shining sun.

"Falken," a voice said beside him. He instantly recognized the voice, and the sound of it filled him with warmth.

He turned his head to the other side to see Domlen sitting next to his bed. The man looked as bad as Falken felt. He was pale and drawn. The lines around his eyes had deepened. His features, already rough, appeared worn...until he smiled. That smile was full of the purest joy.

"You are beautiful when you smile," Falken said.

Domlen leaned forward and kissed him softly. Then he drew back enough to look Falken straight in the eye. "I love you."

The words spread through him like the heat from a roaring fire on a winter day, warming him to his core, making him happier than he had ever been. "I love you so much," he whispered back. "You noble and utterly stubborn fool."

Domlen had the good graces to look abashed. "I suppose I deserve that."

"That and more. But I'm too tired to give you the tongue-lashing you deserve. And I'm too happy." He nodded at Domlen's chest. "How are you?"

Domlen lifted his tunic to reveal his chest. Another large patch of scar tissue marred his skin, this one where he'd stabbed himself with the dagger while trying to save Falken. The wound had healed like a burn. Those scars wouldn't fade.

The sight of them made his heart heavy and brought back memories of the fear, loss, and anger he'd felt toward Domlen for the harm he'd done himself. He understood exactly *why* Domlen had done as he'd chosen, but he also realized he stood at a crossroads. He could feel guilty about not realizing what Domlen intended, or about letting it slip that Domlen had the blood of royalty in his veins, or agonize over his failure to uncover a way to end the spell in time to avoid all that had happened. But he wouldn't. Those things were in the past and couldn't be changed. The simple fact remained, Domlen had given his life and his blood and had broken the curse. And Falken had been there to bring him back from death. He doubted it could've ended so well if they'd planned it that way, but they had won, so he was determined to bite his tongue and accept his own happiness.

"You healed me," Domlen said, leaning forward and taking both Falken's hands and squeezing them. "All of me."

"You bastard," Falken said, tears filling his eyes, despite his decision only an instant ago to let it be and accept his happiness. "Never do that to me again. Never."

Domlen touched his cheek softly, wiping the tears away. There was such compassion in his eyes that Falken had to look away first. "I will never do anything to hurt you ever again."

"Is that a promise?"

"That is my solemn vow."

He nodded, content.

Domlen touched him gently, drawing his attention again. "Are you strong enough to walk? I want to show you something important. I can carry you if needed."

"Can't it wait until after breakfast?"

Domlen smiled. "It will only take a moment. Then we can eat."

"I don't suppose the larder magically filled up with something other than pickled beets and salt mutton."

"Alas, no. But this will be worth it. I promise."

"It had *better* be worth it, because I almost died saving you."

Domlen leaned down and kissed him tenderly. "I know. I love you for it."

The words melted Falken's heart all over again, filling him with warmth that matched any summer day. "And I love you more."

That brought a laugh from the other man. "Are we going to compete over how deeply we love one another?"

"Of course we won't compete. I'm the prince. Therefore I always win."

"We shall see about that," Domlen replied with a raised eyebrow. "Now, my prince, if you will allow me to escort you?"

"I think I can walk, but only if there aren't any stairs. I'm tired of stairs."

Domlen shook his head, grinning. "If there are stairs, I shall carry you, your highness."

"I always preferred 'your worship.'"

"I would not push my luck, Falken."

Climbing out of the warm bedsheets was difficult, but he managed. Domlen helped support him as a wave of dizziness hit him and then slowly passed. As the moment went by, he began to feel stronger, more himself. By the time they left Domlen's chambers and entered the halls, he was walking on his own and his steps were more confident.

The halls were empty and strange now, with strong light blazing in through the windows and pooling on the tiles. Their footsteps echoed. The fortress seemed vast...and still.

"Are they...?" he asked quietly. "Is everyone gone?"

"Not yet. They are waiting on us. Come."

Domlen led him out the main doors into the daylight. He raised a hand to ward off the blazing sunlight. When his vision cleared, he realized he was looking at the tower where he'd been imprisoned. The sides were still streaked with algae and moss, but the places where the sides of the tower showed were brilliant with reflected light. He could imagine what the tower would look like when all its surfaces had been cleaned and restored. It would be a pillar of shining light. A tower afire with brilliance, nearly too bright to look at.

"I believe we can change the name back to the Fortress of the Sun," he murmured.

Domlen smiled and put his arm around his shoulder, standing beside him as they looked out on the courtyard. Falken realized he must have been really dazzled by the tower, because now he could see the courtyard was filled with people. Hundreds of them. Guards, servants, stable hands, and cooks. The captain of the guard, the steward, and Yosel the sage, who watched them with a heartwarming smile on his face. The gathered spirits no longer appeared as they had before. Now they glowed from within, shining with a mellow radiance akin to the sunlight. They were all looking at him, and from them came an aura of peace, of restful happiness and warmth.

"Look," Domlen said, pointing.

Falken turned to look and saw Pilla and Ronev. He had his arm around her shoulder; she had her arm around his waist. They were shining even brighter than the others. When Pilla saw them watching, she smiled shyly, while Ronev raised his free hand in a salute, bringing his fist to his chest. Domlen did the same, saluting him back.

"She wasn't lost forever," Falken whispered. His heart was so full of joy that it felt as though it might burst.

"We freed her spirit from the darkness when we broke the curse. Ronev hasn't left her side for a moment." Domlen turned to him. "They were all waiting for you."

"For me? Why?"

"To thank you. To thank us, together."

As soon as Domlen answered, the gathered spirits began to move forward as one. In another situation, it might have been intimidating to have so many people, much less ghosts, closing in on him. But all he got from the spirits was that gentle aura of peace and safety, compassion and gratitude and love.

Pilla and Ronev reached them first. Pilla was crying. Her tears shimmered and gleamed like polished silver. As the two young lovers came closer, they reached out and touched the prince and the lord of the fortress. As soon as their glowing ethereal hands brushed his skin, the spirits flashed with light and vanished.

"Thank you..." a voice said in Falken's mind. Pilla's voice. "Thank you for all you've done."

He nodded, but she was gone. Ronev was gone. He blinked back tears.

"They're truly gone this time," Domlen said gently. "Free. They are moving on to the afterlife where they can be together."

Then Yosel stood before them. The old man beamed at them like a proud father. "You did it, my young friends. Unconventional, perhaps, but you did it."

"I will miss you, old man," Domlen said, tears on his cheeks.

"And I couldn't have done it without you," Falken added, tears in his eyes and blurring his vision.

"Be happy together," Yosel said. "Always remember what you did for us and what you did for each other."

They both nodded. Then Yosel stepped closer, hugging them both before he vanished in a brilliant flash of warmth and love.

As the other spirits approached, they began to glow brighter before vanishing in bursts of light, leaving him with their voices in his mind, giving thanks, blessing him, wishing the two of them well, or wordlessly conveying their deep gratitude.

At last they all had gone. The courtyard was empty. The sun was shining on the puddles and reflecting from the tower. It was very quiet. As he stared at the clear blue sky, he spotted a bird in the distance. A single bird, far away, but his heart soared with it.

They stood there for a long time, together, feeling the energy still lingering around them. Part of him was having difficulty believing all that had happened. The rest of him never wanted the moment of love and peace to end.

"So…" Domlen finally said. "What happens now?"

"I should be asking you that," he replied. "All I have to do is finish making my escape from this evil castle and return home to my empty life of frivolity, wine, and endless good food. Good, far-better-than-here food." He turned to look Domlen in the eyes, then reached up and drew him into a kiss. "Then again, there's a lot to be said for staying here with you forever."

"We do have wine."

"Enough. You have convinced me."

Domlen's smile spread slowly across his face. It was a beautiful smile. "The storm is over. My people are at peace. We could go anywhere we wished. Do anything we wanted."

Falken kissed him again. His thoughts were spinning quickly through his mind, but he didn't need to think. He knew in his heart what he wanted more than anything else. "I said you convinced me. Now you're making it seem like heaven. No court? No scheming brothers?"

"No life force-stealing phantoms. No rage storms. No rain. We would be free. Together."

"Only the two of us… Whatever would we do?"

"I believe we could think of something to begin with," Domlen said, brushing away a stray lock of Falken's hair.

"Consider me sufficiently tempted. Shall we go inside and get started?"

"Yes."

"Yes, 'your worship.'"

Domlen laughed and kissed him.

Falken decided he loved the man's kisses…almost as much as he loved the sound of his laughter.

~ About the Author ~

A. C. Fox writes m/m fiction and has fallen in love with creating stories of fantasy romance, a longtime pleasure. A. C. works an office job in a tall building with terrible parking and keeps meaning to take the stairs instead of the elevator. Meanwhile, there are plenty of new stories to dream up.

A. C.'s books are *The General's Hostage, The Captive Prince,* and *Hold the Sky.*

~ Also by A. C. Fox ~

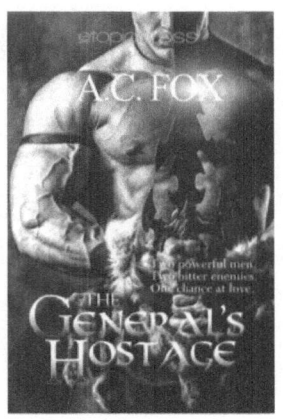

The General's Hostage
The Warriors of Love & Magic Book One
A. C. Fox

Two powerful men. Two bitter enemies. One chance at love.
Tav Cyrdath, a powerful wind adept and a brilliant general, leads the last free humans in a war against the Boa Visk, monsters who have enslaved most of humanity. But when the man who rules Illunvia refuses to surrender, Tav is forced to take the city by sword and magic. Victorious, he intends to execute the human traitor who has done so much harm by defying him. But when the defeated ruler, Duric Darmain, begs him to spare the citizens of Illunvia, Tav finds himself overcome by sudden mercy. He takes the man as a hostage instead, intending to use him in a trap against the

monsters who have set this war in motion. Duric is defeated, broken...and yet Tav can't get his enemy out of his mind. But how could he ever feel this way about a man who has betrayed all Tav stands for?

Duric knows he was only a puppet ruler for the Boa Visk, yet he has done all he can to shield his people from the cruel overlords. Now he is a prisoner, fallen from power, hated and scorned as a traitor. And yet the enemy general begins to treat him with a curious respect and eventually even kindness. He dares not trust again, but this one-time enemy makes him want to yield his heart as hostage, even as he struggles to conquer the fears he can't escape...

Magic can heal wounds, but hearts must be mended with love. Both men have deep scars. Both have seen dark times. But the chance at love exists...if only they can embrace it before the Boa Visk return.

Hold the Sky
AC Fox

When love competes, will anyone win?

Harry has just begun his career as an architect with a well-known Chicago firm, but when he runs up against the talented, successful, not to mention stunningly handsome Garrett Reed, he quickly loses both his cool and his first big contract to the other man. Now a second job has just come up for bid, a huge project that can make Harry's career. And Garrett is after the same prize.

Garrett is fascinated with Harry. He admires the man's drive and talent, not to mention his incredible good looks. But as the wild attraction between them burns hotter, the cool, aloof Garrett finds himself in an uncomfortable position. Can the two of them find a way to temper the passion that flares between them, or will their competitive natures tear their tentative love to pieces?

"Desert Candy" Halloween Heat IV
AC Fox

Halloween Heat IV
Erotic Contemporary M/M Romance

Two hot tales of contemporary gay romance to fill your
goodie bag this Halloween.

"Trex or Treat" by Tara Lain
"Desert Candy" by AC Fox

~ Available Now from Etopia Press ~

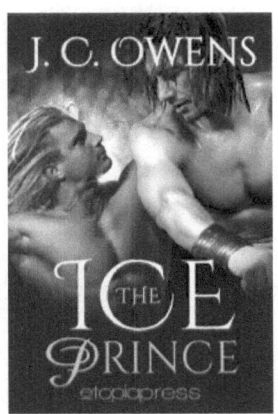

The Ice Prince
J. C. Owens

Honor. Trust. Exile. Will love overcome the lies?

Raised in lies and isolation, denied all knowledge of his family, Aidan awakens one day to find the manor in a state of excitement. Two foreign generals have come for him. They claim he is their long lost prince, the sole survivor of a rebellion that killed the royal family and usurped the throne of Ceratas. And he, Aidan Telan Ameris, is being escorted home to be crowned king.

Naive and submissive he might be, but stupid Aidan is not. Political machinations are something he has never been exposed to, but everything about his upbringing suddenly makes sense. The long hours studying books of history, the training with pistols and swords... He'd been groomed for this moment since his earliest memories. But he knows without a doubt that he's no prince. He's nothing but a pawn in a game he can't possibly understand.

When their carriage is attacked en route to Ceratas, Aiden is taken prisoner by the leader of the rebel forces. General Torin Amaldis Greyan can't help but feel for the poor young man, even if he is the enemy. And soon the heat between them grows to something neither can ignore, something that burns much hotter than warfare.

But nothing is simple in the struggle for Ceratas. There are those who wish to use Aidan to destroy both Torin and his country. When both of them are captured, used against each other to break their wills, Aidan and Torin must find the strength to trust each other in a way neither finds easy, if they're to save each other — and their country...

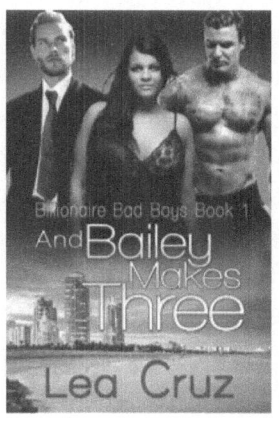

And Bailey Makes Three
Billionaire Bad Boys Book One
Lea Cruz

A threesome with two hot guys might be just the break she needed...

Bailey Castillo is having a horrible Halloween. First, she was fired from her job for no reason by her boss, Doug "the Douchebag" Duchene. Then her friend Ana and her hook-up ditched her at Club Estrella, the exclusive nightclub on Miami's swanky South Beach, leaving the big, beautiful Bailey all alone in her Cat Woman costume with no one to dance with and nothing to do. And now she's drawn the attention of the creepy guy in the cheesy Batman suit, who won't take no for an answer.

That's when she hears the deep, sexy voice behind her—"There you are, precioso mio, I'm sorry I'm late..."—and turns around to face the hottest, sexiest, biggest version of the Terminator she'd ever seen. What else was she supposed to do but reach up and kiss him? And when she can't quite pull her lips from his, and he doesn't pull away either, it isn't as if she can help it. After all, he was rescuing her from Batman. It would be ungrateful not to let him finish his rescue...

But the Terminator — the hot, Latino Diego Rio — wasn't alone. He was there with Noah Wilson, the sexy, blonde male-model type, and the vibes they're sending out suggest they want her. Both of them. Together. Bailey's never had a threesome before, but after the day she's had, a ménage a trois with the gorgeous blonde limo driver and his sexy Cuban lover might just be the universe's way of making it up to her. But when they take her home to the palatial penthouse condo on the beach, Bailey realizes things might not be what they seem, and her two bad-boy lovers might not be who she thinks they are. But how can she think about all that when the sex is just so good…?

Reader note: contains m/m/f ménage elements, BBW and billionaires, interracial/multicultural romance, and male male love